SECRETS, LIES & ALIBIS

WOUNDED HEARTS- BOOK 8

JACQUIE BIGGAR

WAVEFRONT PUBLISHING

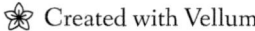

INTRODUCTION

An elusive danger brings two obstinate lovers together for the sake of their unborn child

SAC Agent Amanda Rhinehold is driven to succeed, so it's a bitter pill to swallow when she is forced to accept a demotion in order to distance herself from an error in judgment-- one that leaves her pregnant.

Adam O'Connor uses his playboy image to keep anyone from getting too close. History has shown the people he cares about tends to get hurt, he's like the proverbial bad luck charm. When an affair with his supervisor goes sideways and she leaves town, he figures it's for the best, though his heart isn't so sure.

When trouble comes calling, these two will have to sort their differences in order to protect their baby- and try not to fall in love in the process.

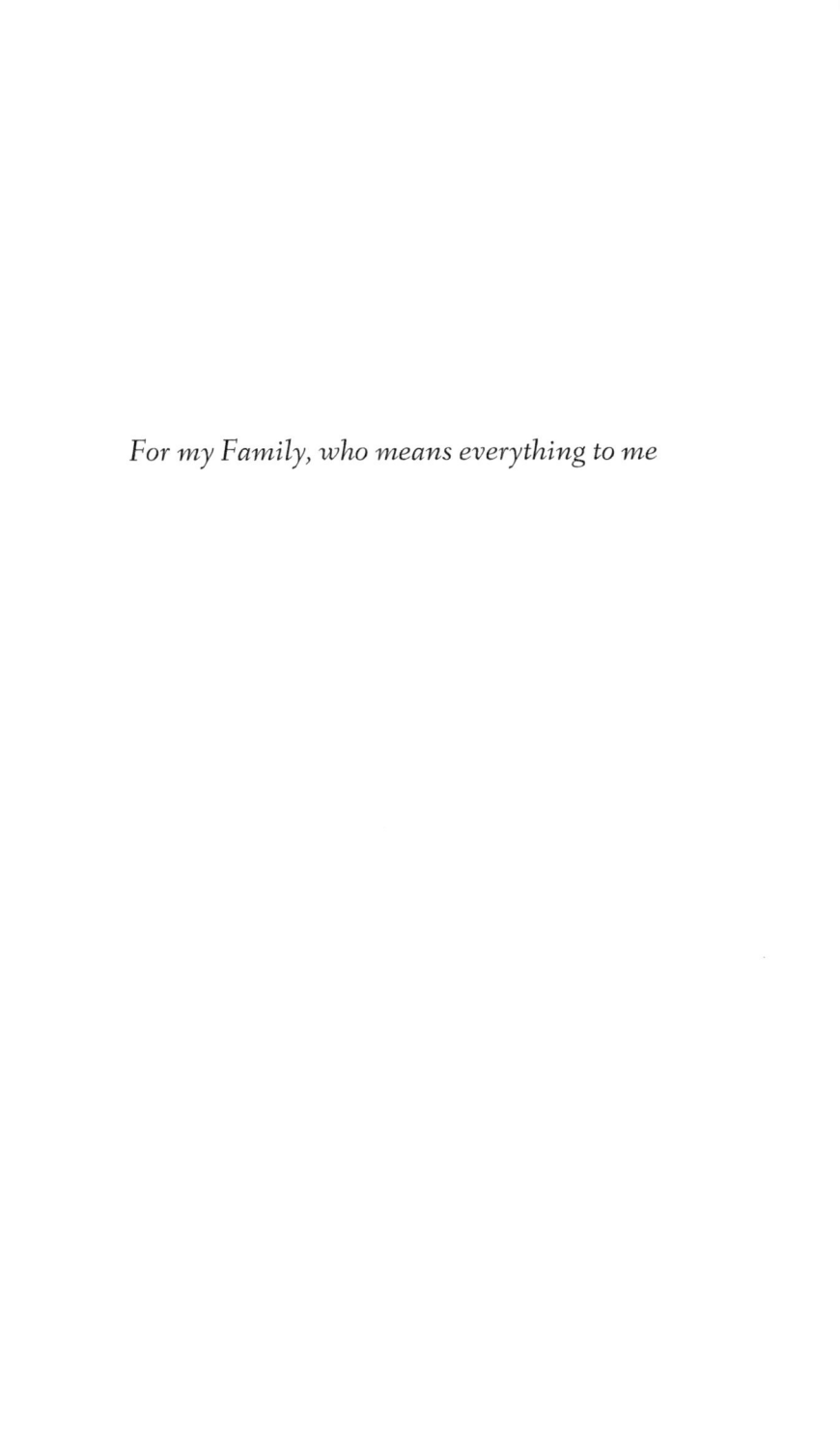

For my Family, who means everything to me

1

Agent Adam O'Connor had been on worse stakeouts. He sat with his new DEA partner in a dark corner of the only bar in Huntersville—the Pickled Pepper—and nursed his soda water. Strangers stood out like hippies at an MIT meeting, and they were getting plenty of sidelong looks. Then again, his partner drew attention without trying.

Brianne Morgan kept watch on the crowd with cool espresso eyes that saw everything. Her clothes were conservative; the white peasant blouse highlighted smooth brown shoulders and a delicate neck while narrow-legged jeans showed off mile-long legs and feet encased in strappy red sandals. Dark ringlets cascaded from the bun on top of her head, tempting a man to wind his fingers in the curls.

Not this man, though. Adam was done with women.

"They should have been here by now," he grumbled into his drink.

"It's only eight o'clock. They aren't even an hour late yet. You need to relax." Agent Morgan smiled, swaying to the honky-tonk music wafting from tinny speakers.

Relax, sure. He'd take that under advisement and file it under *kiss my*—

"There they are," she said, giving a faint nod toward the door.

Three men entered, strutting in as though they owned the place, two rough-looking Hispanics and a tall, wide-shouldered man with close-cut sandy brown hair whose expression said *don't mess with me.*

They sauntered up to the bar and ordered, before turning to eye the crowd. Adam dropped his gaze to his alcohol-free drink and waited for them to lose interest. Except, he'd forgotten he wasn't alone.

"Hey there, *chiquita*, why you sit with that ugly *hombre?*" The youngest of the Hispanics called. He cupped the front of his jeans and thrust out his pelvis while his buddy laughed and chugged on a bottle of beer. "Come see what a real man can teach you."

The American cuffed him on the back of the head and, without waiting to see if they followed, strode to an empty table on the far side of the room, his back to the wall.

Cursing, the young stud straightened his mussed hair,

winked at Brianne, then ambled over to join the tall guy, his buddy trailing behind.

"Shit, next time wear something a little less flashy," Adam snapped.

Brianne raised a brow and stared him down. "Yes, *sir*."

Adam flushed, knowing he'd overreacted. But dammit, they'd—he'd—been on this case far too long to let a dumb mistake jeopardize the whole investigation. If they were recognized as DEA, months of hard work would end up in the toilet.

Truthfully, after having Maggie as his partner for the last five years, it was difficult to transition to a new team member. And then there was Amanda. He still couldn't believe she'd walked away from her position as Special Agent in Charge, never mind turning her back on their blossoming relationship. With all the women in his life giving him a wide berth, it was enough to give a guy a complex.

"What are we looking for?" Brianne murmured, sipping her Bloody Mary.

Adam shuddered. Just looking at the concoction made his stomach roll. "Anything out of the ordinary; a subtle cue from someone else in the bar, anything. If we're really lucky, we'll hit paydirt. Our quarry will get the call we've all been waiting for and we can wrap this thing up with a pretty bow and go home."

Except home was a lonely place to be when your only companion is regret.

"Hold your positions. I repeat, hold your positions. Fox is entering the henhouse. Eyes on the prize, Agents."

Adam rolled his eyes at the voice of the acting commander in his earpiece. The guy was stiff as a board, and about as *by the rulebook* as could be—it made his jaw ache. At least with Amanda... it didn't matter, she'd left him. He had to make do, like it or not.

A nondescript man walked in, brown hair, dark eyes, medium build, mid-thirties. He carefully surveyed the other clientele—a couple of cowboys playing pool and an old drunk mumbling into his glass—then took a stool at the bar, near the American and his group.

"This is our guy. Ready to do your part, Morgan?"

Brianne tensed, staring at the cell phone resting on the table.

"Just a quick bump and grab, you've got this. I'll be right here in case anything goes wrong—which it won't," Adam assured her.

She nodded and rose, phone in hand, and took on a wobbly half-drunk persona. "What's a girl gotta do to get a drink around here?" she whined, whipping around on unsteady legs to make her way to the bar. "Never mind, I'll get my own."

Adam, and every other male in the building, watched her wiggle her butt up to the counter, right next to Mr. Plain and Ordinary, who looked distinctly uncomfortable and leaned away from the tottering female.

"I need a drink," she demanded, slapping her hand on the counter. "Service suuuucks here," she confided, half-laying against the stranger.

"Ease up," Adam warned through the earpiece as Mr. P and O pushed her upright, his face grim. "You're coming on too heavy."

The bartender came from the back room, a towel in hand, and started toward Brianne. "Get out of there," Adam ordered. "Now, Agent Morgan."

Brianne straightened and giggled. "Never mind, my favorite song just started." With that, she wandered away from the bar, arms akimbo and hips swaying hypnotically to Deana Carter's "Strawberry Wine".

The American frowned and shook his head, and Adam could only agree. Brianne Morgan was a daredevil. His heart was drumming like crazy, but, surprisingly, the adrenaline was like welcoming an old friend.

He grinned and rose to meet her, taking her in his arms and swinging her toward the door. "C'mon, sweetheart, time for bed."

The two Hispanics whistled and stomped their feet, signaling their approval while the bartender eyed them suspiciously. As long as he kept quiet about the lack of alcohol in their drinks...

"Whew, that was fun," Brianne chirped as soon as they were in the clear. "I thought he was going to blow my cover."

"You took unnecessary risks," Adam growled. "What would you have done if he called you out on your little act?"

She shrugged, unrepentant. "I'd have thought of something. Anyway, I got it." She opened her hand to reveal the cell phone in her palm, and grinned. "Someone's going to be angry when he realizes his phone has been switched."

Adam accepted the gadget and started toward the car. "Now to get our resident tech guru to find out the information we need before he locks it down."

Getting into the driver's side, he gave in to curiosity and lifted the phone for inspection. This was it, he could feel it. "Wish you were here, Amanda," he whispered.

2

A manda Rhinehold glared at the computer screen on her desk and rubbed her swollen belly. A rain/snow mix fell in a gray sheet beyond the fifth story window of her office at the DEA Headquarters in Springfield, Virginia adding to her gloominess.

Jan stopped in the doorway. "If there's one thing you can count on in Springfield, it's the rain." She chuckled and nodded toward the investigation Amanda was working on. "How's it going?"

Amanda shrugged. "Not as fast as I want it to with this little guy on the way." She glanced down and grimaced. Eight months ago, she would never have guessed her life would change to such a degree.

Jan gave her a commiserating smile. "It sounds as though you need a night on the town. Want to try that new Italian place Tom and I went to for our anniversary?"

"Thanks, but I better stick around and try to get this report finished. The director wants it done yesterday." Normally, she was a workaholic, but ever since she'd left Texas—and Adam O'Connor—behind, she couldn't seem to focus.

"Okay, well, give me a call if you change your mind. I guess I better get back out there, someone needs to keep this office running smoothly." Jan grinned and disappeared from view.

Amanda rose and rounded her utilitarian desk to close the door, blocking the hum of voices from down the hall. Jan had joked, but it was true. Director Kincade was demanding, and Jan, as his Administrative assistant, had her hands full.

She turned and leaned against the door, sighing as she stared at the four walls, empty except for the plain black frame holding her certification. She wandered over and carefully straightened the picture, though it wouldn't be long before she'd be taking it down to pack away with her badge—maybe forever.

The sky had darkened considerably. She glanced at the delicate silver watch on her wrist to see it was after four and rubbed her baby bump again. The little munchkin had been on the move all day, disrupting her concentration. The closer her due date came, the more she wished for the impossible—to have the baby's father by her side. A feeling akin to home-sickness swept over her.

"It's just the nesting urge," she told the baby. "I read

about it in all those pregnancy books I picked up from the library. Maybe this weekend, we'll go and pick out your crib and start decorating the spare bedroom. What do you think?"

A foot kicked her hand and she gasped, warmth flooding her chest. "I guess that's a yes?" She laughed. "Boy or girl, I think you have a future as a soccer player." For some reason, she'd decided to wait until the baby arrived to find out the sex. It meant playing it safe with her color scheme, but she was okay with that. Mint green and butter yellow were happy colors and she needed some of that in her life right now.

Her cell phone rang, the tone one she set for personal calls. Frowning, Amanda strode to her desk to retrieve the call. There were only a few people with her number, could it be—?

Annie Martin's cute pixie face lit up the screen.

Refusing to acknowledge the disappointment, she hit the video reply button and smiled as her friend came online. "Checking up on me again?" Annie had taken to calling weekly in the past month or so, "*Just to chat.*"

"Hello to you, too," Annie said good-naturedly. "Actually, Sara Kelley has been teaching a painting class here at The Craft Shack and I wanted to show you what I made." The camera view switched to a wall lined up with various watercolor projects with varying degrees of competency.

"Well, what do you think?" She swung the camera to her face and back again, making Amanda grab for the desk.

"I think you're making me dizzy," she complained, dropping into her chair. "Which one is yours?"

"This one, silly. I thought you would recognize it." The camera focused in on print near the bottom of the wall. A scarred wooden stool sat in the center of a round woven carpet, its weaving done in shades of blue, green, and yellow. But it was the baseball cap thrown carelessly on the seat that took Amanda's breath away. A Red Sox cap.

"How did you know?" she whispered, caught up in a flood of Adam-filled memories. His cognac-brown eyes, thick blond hair, wide shoulders—the feel of his mouth on hers.

Annie flipped the camera, her worried expression coming into focus. "Oh, no, Amanda. I didn't mean to upset you. Jared said Adam wore that cap all the time and I thought you might like it for the baby's room—you know, as a keepsake. I'm such an idiot."

Amanda shook her head, even as her pulse tripped through her veins. "No, you're not. It's a sweet gesture, really. The color is perfect, too. You have some talent there." She hid her agitation behind a smile. "Sara must be a good teacher."

An obviously relieved Annie grinned into the phone. "She's the best. Her art show in Spokane last month drew some serious collectors. We're lucky to have her."

Over the months since they'd left the Texas ranch where

Amanda had been shot in the line of duty and lost her heart to a fellow agent, Annie had kept in touch and their unlikely friendship had grown.

"Maybe after the baby is born, we'll surprise you with a visit. You've told me so much about Tidal Falls it feels as though I've been there already."

Annie's eyes lit up. "Oh, yes, you must. You know we'd love to have you. Jared's busy with his and Nick's new private investigator business, and Chris is at the age where hanging with his mother isn't cool—" she chuckled, "so, that leaves me and Daniel, who's growing like a bean stock. I'd forgotten how active toddlers are, he gets into everything."

Amanda glanced down at her own baby bump. "Don't tell me that, I'm overwhelmed enough, as is." She made a mental note to get more books from the library, this time on the toddler years.

A bell tinkled in the background and Annie sighed. "Time to get back to work, I'm afraid. If you're okay with it, I'll package this painting up and get Jared to mail it off to you —consider it my baby shower gift. Next time we talk, it'll almost be your due date, squee! Okay, gotta go, love you."

The screen went blank, leaving the room quiet, yet filled with the lingering warmth of her friend's parting words. It took a moment for her to digest the fact that Jared would have her address and could conceivably pass it on to his friend, Adam.

She opened the phone to call Annie back, then changed

her mind. Annie was busy, and even if Jared did say something to Adam, it was doubtful he would do anything about it. After all, he hadn't made an effort to track her down so far. Sooner or later, she would have to tell him about the child, but that conversation could wait. She was better off on her own.

A TWINGING BACK pain halted the progress Amanda had made with the investigation she'd been working on. Stretching out the kinks, she read over the Henderson County, Tennessee police report.

A THP trooper had pulled over a tractor-trailer rig for a traffic violation and, while performing a routine vehicle safety inspection, came across several discrepancies in the shipping manifest. Calling for backup, the troopers searched the trailer and found unaccounted boxes heavily wrapped in cellophane which contained sealed bags of cocaine and marijuana with a street value of over five million. The truck was found to have travelled from New York.

There were many more busts like this spread throughout the country. Sometimes, it seemed as though they were up against insurmountable odds.

The focus of her investigation was on the method of transporting these drugs. While in Texas, her team had been tasked with stopping an incoming shipment of methamphetamines and weapons arriving from Mexico via cattle trucks. Working that case—and subsequently getting shot—she'd also learned of two escaped convicts from Canada, with ties to the same anarchist movement, who used a semi to disappear into the USA.

She didn't believe in coincidences. There was a link between the trucking companies and the crimes; she just had to find it.

"Rhinehold, what are you still doing here?"

Amanda jumped at the sound of Director Kincaid's booming voice. He stood in her doorway, his perpetual frown making him look like an annoyed hound dog.

"Sorry, sir, I was busy and didn't realize the time." She glanced at her watch, surprised to see it was after eight. "I'll just finish up this report and be on my way."

"I need you at your best, Agent. Go home. There's nothing on your desk that can't wait for a few hours."

She opened her mouth to argue the point, but another uncomfortable twinge in her back changed her mind. "Thank you, sir," she said, shifting awkwardly.

Instead of leaving as she'd expected, the director waited at the door while she hurried to save her files and close down the computer before gathering the black leather clamshell purse she kept in the bottom drawer and her down-filled three-quarter length jacket with faux fur collar from the coat tree in the corner behind her desk. After her time in Las

Vegas and the months in Texas, the chilly Virginia winter was making itself felt.

"Have you lived in Springfield long, sir?" she asked, wrapping a woolly purple scarf around her neck as they walked down the now quiet hallway. It was different from what she was used to out in the field. There, work had been the priority for her team. In the Intelligence Research Specialist Division, it was more about coordinating task forces, analyzing information, pattern analysis, and cyber investigations. They used all the raw data to combat drug trafficking and organized crime—satisfying, if not as exciting.

"Twenty years," he answered, punching the elevator down button with a jab of his finger. "Met my wife eighteen years ago, married her six months later, and had two kids—a boy and a girl—shortly thereafter." He glanced at her basketball-shaped stomach. "First one?"

"That obvious?" she replied with a smile.

They stepped into the elevator car and the doors slid closed. "I noticed the baby books on your desk. My wife practically haunted the bookstores before Jed was born. When Amy came along, she was much more relaxed. Parking level?" He raised a bushy eyebrow and waited, his hand hovering over the keypad.

"Hmm? Oh, Main floor, thank you. I take the transit home." As the elevator dropped down the shaft, she closed her eyes and tried to keep the roller coaster feeling to a minimum.

"Nervous in enclosed spaces?" Kincaid inquired, sympathy in his voice.

Amanda gripped the railing at her back and gave a faint nod. "I was stuck in one once as a child—never did get over it." After the baby came, she planned on getting her exercise by taking the stairs.

"Agent Rhinehold—"

She tensed and looked over to see him fiddling with his tie. "Yes, sir?"

He straightened as the elevator came to a stop and the door opened on the Main floor facing an imposing glass entrance. A security guard glanced their way and lifted a hand in greeting. Kincaid pressed his thumb on the hold door button and met her gaze. "I thought you should know, the suspect who shot you in Texas, he was released after his hearing and failed to report to his bail supervisor. When the peace officers checked his address, they found he'd cleared out without paying his rent."

Amanda's heart plummeted faster than the elevator car had done. "Are you telling me he's in the wind?"

"Yes, Agent. That's exactly what I'm telling you."

3

Stepping out of the shower in his hotel room, Adam used a hand towel to clear the foggy mirror and rubbed his palm over the stubble covering his chin. He should probably shave, but instead turned away to check his cell phone resting on the edge of the sink. Still no word on the results of their sting operation from two days ago. *Damn it*, they were on a time crunch—what was taking so long?

Frustration drove him into the main room. He tossed the phone onto the unused twin of his queen bed and sank down to dry off and get dressed. Patience wasn't his strong suit and sitting around waiting for Clark to hack into their quarry's phone was driving him nuts.

His laptop sat on the desk next to the oversized television. He briefly debated catching up on some emails and working on the report SAC Thomas was waiting for, but was too restless to give it his full attention. Instead, he picked up his phone and called an old friend.

"Hey, beautiful. Are you ready to leave that ugly cowboy and come on the road with me?"

His former partner, Maggie Holt, laughed, her voice lifting the weight from his chest. "That *ugly* cowboy is sitting right beside me and the phone is on speaker."

"Good thing I know you have a secret man-crush on me, O'Connor, or we'd be having words," Frank Stein growled.

It was Adam's turn to chuckle. "And here I thought I hid it so well, Chief. How's farm life?" He rose and strode over to the heavy brown drapes covering the second-floor window, pushing them aside to stare at the half-empty parking lot. "You forgot to mention how dead this hole-in-the-wall town is, or I might have begged your mom to let me stay."

"You know my door is open any time, buddy. Just keep your lascivious thoughts about my woman to your—oomph," he ended on a gasp.

"You'll have to forgive Frank. He's been acting like a neanderthal lately. We're working on it, aren't we darling?" Maggie cooed.

Adam couldn't believe the difference in his friend and one-time lover. After the horrors she'd endured as a captive in a human smuggling ring, he'd worried she would never fully recover, but her newfound relationship with Master

Chief Frank Stein had changed her life. He was happy for them, if envious.

"I've little doubt you'll have him toeing the line in no time," he said aloud. "You always kept me in my place—while we worked together," he hurried to add. The last thing he wanted to do was cause any friction between the lovebirds.

"If you two are done denigrating my character, is there a reason for this phone call or are you just bored and looking for someone to pick on?" Frank asked, hitting the nail on the proverbial head.

Adam shook his head and grinned. There was no putting anything over on the Chief. "Truthfully, I'm going out of my mind in this hotel room. If I buy the beer, will you do the cooking?"

"You got it buddy, see you in a few," Frank agreed.

"And bring your new partner along," Maggie added. "I want to see who's watching your back while I'm on leave."

A picture of Agent Morgan formed in his mind. Young, vivacious, determined. Mags would eat her alive.

"I think she's busy getting her hair done, or something," he prevaricated, cringing at the lame excuse.

The line quieted for a couple of moments and he strained to hear the muffled conversation on the other end.

"*He's a big boy.*" This from Frank.

"*I'm worried about him,*" Mags replied.

More back-and-forthing, then Maggie came on again, her

tone resolute. "Dinner's at six, bring the agent, Adam. I'm not taking no for an answer. And by the way, Frank's brother will be here, too, so buy extra beer." She hung up before he could say anything else, though truthfully, it didn't matter. If he didn't take Brianne out to meet her, Maggie would just find another way to run into her. It was better if they got it over with in the relative secrecy of the ranch. That way, they'd have room to bury the body.

ADAM TURNED into the Bella Vista ranch yard two hours later and the stress of the last few days melted away. The sky had changed from crystal blue to sapphire on the drive, but men still hurried back and forth, finishing the day's chores before going home to one of the many workers' cabins dotting the area. The acre-long red barn that dominated the yard was lit from within, the light a beacon in the dark.

"Is that him?" Brianne asked in a hushed whisper.

Frank had appeared in the entrance of the big building, but where the sheer size of the barn should have dwarfed the man, it only highlighted the broad width of his shoulders and tree trunks for legs.

"That's the Chief," he agreed with a grin, swinging to a stop at the base of the hill leading up to the farmhouse. He looked at her nervous expression in the dashboard lights. "Ready?"

"You didn't tell me he would be so... intimidating."

He raised a brow, surprised. "This coming from the woman who took on a bar filled with drug dealers and didn't bat an eye?"

"Yeah, well, they didn't look like him," she retorted, climbing out of the car in thigh-high red velvet boots that matched her body-hugging wrap-around dress and woolen coat.

He'd wondered at her choice of clothing, considering where they were going, but now it made sense. She'd dressed herself in feminine armor; Brianne wasn't the tough girl she made herself out to be—interesting.

He followed her from the car and led the way across the distance to greet his friend. "Frank, good to see you."

Frank took his hand in a firm grip. "It's been a while. Maggie was getting ready to go into town and chase you down."

Adam resisted the urge to scrunch his shoulders at the reprimand. "I'm glad she didn't. I'd never forgive myself if something happened to her."

"Likewise, my brother, likewise." Frank turned his attention to Brianne hovering in the background. "Ma'am." He doffed his hat.

Brianne flushed and practically batted her lashes. "I've heard a lot about you, Mr. Stein."

Frank raised a brow at Adam. He shrugged in return. "Your fame precedes you, Chief, what can I say?"

"A little less comes to mind," Frank said before turning to Brianne. "Maggie is up at the house. She's anxious to meet you. Shall we?" He lifted a hand to someone in the barn, then gestured for them to start the trek up the hill. "Have you been an agent for long, Miss...?"

"Brianne is fine. Brianne Morgan. No, sir, this is my first assignment. I'm a quick study, though," she added defensively, shooting a warning glare at Adam.

"She's impetuous," Adam corrected.

"And, of course, you know nothing about that, being the level-headed SEAL that you are—I mean were." Frank smirked.

How did this end up being about my past mistakes? "Once a SEAL, always a SEAL." Adam looked at his friend and the flare of anger faded away. "If not for you and my Team brothers, I'd be dead. Which is why I know how important it is to obey orders, *Agent Morgan*." His tone suggested she pay attention. "Mistakes can cost not only your life, but potentially that of your partner, or even worse, a civilian. It's up to us to stay ahead of a bad situation before it goes sideways, and innocents pay the price—understand?"

Brianne's chin rose, but she didn't contradict him for once. "Yes, sir." She dug in her considerable heels and surged up the rest of the hill but came to a sudden halt when the tall figure of a man rose from the shadows on the porch.

Adam glanced at Frank. "Did he know we were coming?"

Frank shrugged and started up the stairs. "He does now."

Wonderful. Adam joined Brianne and leaned close to whisper. "I'll explain later," just as Frank's brother Cameron stepped into the light shining from inside the home.

"It's the drug buyer," Brianne hissed, her hands clenching as though wishing she had a weapon.

Obviously, there was nothing wrong with either Frank or Cam's hearing. Both men stared down at them from their lofty height, one with a knowing smile, the other with a grim expression.

"What do you mean, *drug buyer?*" Frank growled.

"Well, I guess that cat is out of the bag," Cam said equitably. "I could use a beer, anyone else?" He'd just reached for the screen when Maggie opened the door and looked at each of them in turn, her gaze lingering on Brianne the longest.

"It's November, are you waiting for an engraved invitation or are you getting yourselves in here before Emily comes out to drag you in by the ear?"

Frank's expression underwent a metamorphosis, changing from drill sergeant to sap in about two seconds flat. "Hi, honey, I'm home." His tone was low, intimate. It told anyone who was listening that *she* was his reason for living.

A ghost of the green monster skittered over Adam's heart, but the change he saw in both of his friends helped him bat the jealousy away. Maggie hadn't been his in a long time. He was glad she'd found love with the Chief—they deserved some happiness.

She stepped out, shawl wrapped around her shoulders, midnight dark hair picking up the glow from the lights behind her, and gave Frank a lingering kiss before turning to her guests. "Supper is almost ready. Come in and warm up. I want to hear everything."

Adam's frown matched the one forming on Frank's face. "Mags, you know we can't talk shop with you anymore. You're a civilian now, remember?" He'd been stunned when she'd turned in her gun and badge a few months ago, but secretly relieved. After her ordeal, she'd lost her resolve. It could have gotten her killed.

Maggie put her hands on her hips and stared him down. "Adam O'Connor, don't even start with me. I've been sitting out here going slowly mad wondering how you're doing with the case. You'd better not think you're going to talk about the weather, or I'll tell your new partner all your bad habits."

Cam chuckled. "This should be an interesting dinner."

Adam met Frank's warning look and swore under his breath. Interesting wasn't the half of it.

4

Cameron sipped his beer and quietly observed the unusual gathering sitting down to a meal at his parents' dinner table. He rubbed callused fingers over gouges he'd made in the wood as a kid. So much had changed in the fifteen years since he'd been gone, yet this old table his father had built by hand still stood the test of time.

Momma laughed at something Spencer said, her eyes sparkling under the crystal chandelier—a new addition to the home. His brother had mentioned the foreman was courting their mother, but Cam hadn't believed it until he'd seen it with his own eyes. They made an unlikely pair; the grizzled farmhand and the prim and proper lady-of-the-manor, but as long as Spence made her happy, that's all that mattered.

Spencer brandished his fork in the air, a tempting morsel of steak dangling from the tines as he shared one of his greatly embellished tales with the pretty DEA agent, Brianne Morgan. She glanced over to Cam's end of the table as though she'd felt his attention on her and raised a delicate brow over mysterious teak-brown eyes. He replied by tipping his bottle in a mock salute, a smile lingering on his lips. She jerked her attention back to the story, her spine stiff. His humor faded. She had a temper. Normally, he liked women with feisty attitudes, but not in dangerous situations. Her impetuous decisions could have ruined months of hard labor, and possibly cost them the investigation. He wanted her off the case—like yesterday.

Frank sat at the head of the table, Maggie on his right. He looked so much like their father, it made Cam's heart clench. To think his brother had left the ranch—something he never would have expected—and became a Navy SEAL. He'd asked him about it a couple of times, but so far, Frank was living up to the image of a stoic cowboy. Then again, he was close-lipped about his life story, as well, so there was that—

"You're not saying much," Adam murmured, as though he'd read Cam's mind.

Cam shrugged, unwilling to give voice to the emotional cauldron brewing in his gut. Coming home was stirring up embers he'd rather keep doused. "Just takin' it all in, you know?"

Adam nodded, his gaze drifting to Maggie and away

again. "Sure, I get it. In our line of work, we need to enjoy the downtime whenever we get the chance. Speaking of which—"

"Not here," Cam interrupted. He had no wish to embroil his family in the mess going on practically in their backyard.

"What are you two arguing about?" Maggie asked, her gaze curious and concerned at the same time.

Adam frowned, but turned an amiable smile on the women. "I was trying to convince Cameron to grab me a beer, but he insists that after my first visit to the ranch I'm not company anymore—in other words, I can get my own." He laughed.

Emily tsked, tsked, and hurried into the kitchen, returning with a frosty bottle in hand. She passed it to an embarrassed O'Connor who mumbled his thanks, then stopped at Cam's side, her frame diminutive next to his. "You may not be a boy any longer, but you can't outgrow manners. I taught you better than that."

"Yes, ma'am," he said, his voice low, aware that the conversation around the table had died. Kind of like he wished he could do right now. How could he be in his thirties and still feel like a grounding was in his imminent future?

"That's better," Emily said, patting his shoulder before resuming her seat. She smiled at Brianne. "So, Brianne— what a lovely name—have you been seeing our Adam very long? He's a charmer that one, you'll have a job getting him to toe the line."

"Ma." Frank shook his head in consternation. "The stuff that comes out of your mouth."

"What?" she asked, affronted. "I was just asking a simple question, that's all." She forked a ripe cherry tomato from her plate and took a bite.

Cam grinned, happy to have the attention on someone else. Besides, he wouldn't mind hearing Brianne-with-the-lovely-name's answer, either—just for informational purposes.

"They're working together," Maggie inserted, her sympathetic gaze on Adam. "Brianne is Adam's new partner now that I've retired from the organization."

Frank took her hand and gave it a gentle squeeze. "And I, for one, am glad you did. Now I get to boss you around the ranch twenty-four-seven."

She rewarded him with a saucy look that promised retribution. "We'll see about that," she murmured before turning to Cam. "See what I have to put up with? When are you going to move back home so that I have an ally?"

His mom stilled, the tomato suspended on her fork. Spencer looked up from his plate of food, another crease adding to the roadmap on his forehead. Frank... Frank stared at him with his heart in his goddamn eyes, making the ball in Cam's throat a bomb set to explode.

Amazingly, it was Brianne who came to his rescue. She

giggled, as though Maggie had just imparted the funniest punchline she'd ever heard. "I'm not sure people in his line of work make very good allies."

"His line of work?" Emily asked, setting the fork down to press a closed fist to her chest. "Cameron, I thought you said you were a salesman? That you have to travel all over the country for your job. What is this girl saying?"

So much for thinking she was his savior. Cam shot a thanks-for-nothing glare at Brianne before rising to circle the table and crouch at his mother's side. "Ma, there's something I should have told you months ago, when I first returned to Texas, but I couldn't, I was sworn to silence." He grasped her delicate, arthritic hand and cursed the years he'd wasted.

She looked at him with a wounded expression. "We are your family and yet you walked away from us without a backward glance. Now, this many years later, we welcomed you back, no questions asked—and yet you lied to us." She tugged her hand free and rose, her shoulders quivering. "I don't think I want to hear the reason you would hurt your mother and brother that way. If you'll excuse me, I'm going to rest for a while. I don't feel too well."

She left the room with her head high, but Cam had seen the tears trailing down her cheeks and he felt like shit. She was right, what kind of son did that? *One who felt he didn't have a choice.*

He rose, intending to follow her and try to explain the

unexplainable, but Spencer stopped him with a hand on his arm.

"Leave her be, son. She needs some space. I'll check on her in a bit." He squeezed Cam's arm, then let him go. "Who's ready for pie?"

5

Amanda left the transit station shivering. Big, fat flakes of driving snow had started to fall about halfway home, and now it was piling up, making the sidewalks treacherous. Huddling into her coat, she tugged the hat that matched her scarf over her ears, and tiptoed through the drifts, blinking snow from her lashes. She was sorry now she hadn't accepted the director's offer of a ride.

Cars squelched past, sending a mini blizzard to batter exposed skin and cake her clothes in a heavy, wet slush. The brownstone she'd rented was only five blocks from the station, but it felt like twenty in this weather. At least, at this time of night, she appeared to be the only one walking, so she didn't have to fight for sidewalk space. It didn't help that the tram seemed to stop at every station between downtown and her destination, adding a good forty-five minutes to the already hour-long trip. She should really look into buying a car, especially with the baby on the way, but city driving wasn't her thing. There were two types of drivers; the over-cautious, brake-for-everything kind, and the type who thought city streets were meant for Indy driving. She was firmly in the second column. It drove her crazy to get behind some old codger creeping along at twenty-miles-an-hour in a fifty zone. When she had caught herself giving in to road rage, Amanda decided it was time to get out from behind the wheel before someone got hurt. It hadn't mattered in Las Vegas where there were buses, taxi companies, and ride share; getting around wasn't an issue. Springfield was taking a while to get used to, or maybe it was because she really didn't want to be here.

Her heart was in Texas.

She slipped, wrenching her back. "Ow," she cried, trying to regain her balance. Why, oh why, did she have to wear stylish shoes instead of sturdy boots? The tears that were never far away streamed down her cheeks, frustrating her with her weakness. She dashed them away with cold, trembling fingers. "I'm tired, that's all. A hot bath will be good for both of us, Sweet Pea. Just a little farther..."

Rounding the corner, her stomach plunged to her frozen toes. Two police cruisers, red and blue lights flashing, were parked in the middle of the block—right in front of her house.

Had there been a break in? Fire? *Adam?*

Fear put wings on her feet. She hurried down the street, ignoring the icy walk and her aching back. Her door stood ajar, an officer on the stoop keeping watch. She was briefly annoyed with the heat loss, until the reality of what she might face hit her.

"What's going on here?" She panted, stress making her breathless.

The sergeant held up a hand, stopping her at the gate.

"Is this your home, Ma'am?" He glanced inside, then stepped down to meet her.

"Yes," she said irritably, craning her neck to see over his shoulder. "Is it a robbery? What did they take?" She tried to brush past, but he held firm, taking up the entry.

"Hold on, there. I need to see some I.D. and ask a few questions first. Name, please?" He held a black notebook and pen, waiting for her answer.

"Oh, for Pete's—" She cut herself off, aware he was doing his job, and dug in her bag for her wallet. Holding up her badge, she said, "Special Agent Amanda Rhinehold with the DEA. Now, will you tell me what is going on here or do I need to get hold of your superior?"

He startled her by flashing a light over first the identification and then her face, before nodding and stepping aside to let her past. "Sorry, Ma'am, you can go in now. Oh, here, put these on." He handed her a set of disposable booties and latex gloves. "And please, don't touch anything until the crime techs are done." He keyed the mic hooked to his pocket and said a few words while she walked forward in a daze.

The lock was jimmied, the paint scuffed like a crowbar may have been used to force the door. Stopping long enough to step into the booties and tug on the tight-fitting gloves, she pushed open the door and took stock of the entry. The oval mirror over the hall table was spiderwebbed, with a big chunk missing from the middle as though someone had taken their temper out on the inanimate object. Dirty wet puddles marred the cream tile, whether from the police or the perps it was hard to say until they had a timeline. She'd been gone since early morning; it could have happened at any time.

Someone had broken into her home.

Amanda shivered, then straightened her spine. She had to hold herself together until the police left. Treading carefully, she edged down the hallway toward the noise coming from her office behind the stairs.

The wanton destruction took her aback; couch cushions slashed, bookcase overturned, pictures ripped off the walls, and her computer... The desktop lay on the floor, the screen as shattered as her emotions. Who would do this?

"Ma'am, are you okay?" A handsome young officer who looked wet behind the ears glanced up from the digital camera he'd been using to photograph the crime scene.

Her house, a crime scene. Amanda bit her lip to hold back the hysterical laughter. Ten years with the DEA and she'd never been threatened—until now.

"Ma'am?" he repeated, eyeing his partner nervously. She barely glanced around, her attention on the damaged computer.

"Yes, yes, I'm fine," Amanda said impatiently, donning her mantle of aloofness. *"Never let them see you sweat,"* her old mentor had warned. "Is the hard drive intact?"

The cop rose, shaking her head. "Hard to tell until our lab guys can check it out." Her eyes were a flat blue, analytical. "Mind telling us why someone would risk a daytime robbery of your home, Agent...?"

"Rhinehold," Amanda supplied, aware she was facing hours of interrogation and suddenly too tired to stand for much longer. "I have no idea. I don't keep anything of value here, other than the work I do on the computer, and yes, it's encrypted." Didn't mean the thieves couldn't hack into it, though. If they could hold governments hostage, what chance did she have? At least she'd had the sense to download the most sensitive material to a flash drive which she carried with her at all times.

But her contact list was on her computer. Dammit. None of the undercover agents used their real names, of course, but it was still classified, and could be dangerous in the wrong hands.

She was going to have to face her past, like it or not.

ADAM KEPT his gaze averted and offered the Steins as much privacy as he could in the crowded dining room. Family squabbles gave him hives. Coming from a broken home, he knew all about the damage secrets could do.

"Keep me company?" Maggie asked, touching his hand to get his attention. She gazed at him sympathetically and nodded toward the outside deck.

He smiled, grateful for a way out of the awkward situation. "Any time, any place." Grabbing his beer, he followed her out the door, aware of more than one pair of eyes drilling into his back.

"So... that was interesting," He took up a post against the railing and shook his head. "And you thought chasing bad guys was tough."

Maggie's laugh was sultry, like the woman. She wandered over to the white-washed swing and took a seat. "It wasn't easy, that's for sure, and to answer your unasked question, yes, I miss it. But not enough to go back." She set the chair swaying. "I'm happy, Adam. Maybe for the first time in a very long time."

"Wow, thanks a lot," he sputtered. "Guess I've been put in my place." He took a swig of beer, trying, and failing, to wash the sour taste of regret away.

She sighed, bringing the swing to a jarring halt. "You know what I mean, Obi-Dramatic-One. It wasn't you, it was me—and how corny does that sound?"

Even though she'd bruised his heart, he sat beside her

and cupped her hand in his. "Not corny, at all. I hate to admit it, but we were better partners than lovers. I have too much baggage for any meaningful relationships, and you..." He kissed her fingertips. "You deserve more." He grinned as Frank came through the door like an avenging angel. "Chief."

"O'Connor. Trying to steal my woman again?" Frank crossed his arms, biceps flexing, and rocked back on his heels.

Maggie chuckled and rose, jasmine scenting the air. "So, I'm *your* woman, am I?" She trailed her fingers over his chest, then pinched his arm.

"Ouch," he grumbled, rubbing the opposite arm. "Damn skeeters."

"Don't start thinking you can go all Neanderthal on me, Frank Stein. I'm my *own* woman, and don't you forget it." She stood on her toes to give him a long, lingering kiss, then turned and winked at Adam. "Now that we have that settled, I'm going to warn your new partner about your idiosyncrasies. I'll send Cameron out with more beer, be gentle with him, will you?"

"Gentle with him?" Frank's brow rose. "What about me?"

Adam chortled as Maggie strutted inside. "Never thought I'd see the day the great Frank Stein would be brought low by love—it's kinda sweet."

Frank snorted. "The only thing sweet around here is Momma's cherry pie, which I missed out on with all the drama. I warned Cam to talk to her. Secrets have a way of hurting those we love the most and our family seems to have made a career of doing just that."

He moved to the railing and stared out at the dusky fields. "Do you have many regrets, O'Connor?"

Amanda's beautiful, resolute face came to mind. She'd told him their affair had prompted the decision to give up her position as Special Agent in Charge of their unit, and transfer to another part of the country. And then there was his failure to save Maggie from the hands of a madman. Or the time he almost got his SEAL Team killed... yeah, he had regrets. Too many to count.

"A few," he admitted aloud, his voice raspy. "Why do you ask?"

Frank turned and leaned against the rail, silver eyes glinting in the dark. "I'm worried about Cam," he said bluntly. "He may be back in our lives, but it's only peripheral. He's not the same."

"Did you really expect him to be?" Adam shook his head. "C'mon, Chief, he's not your kid brother anymore."

Frank slammed his hand down, rattling the railing. "Yeah, well, that's on me, isn't it?"

"And who made you God?" Cam demanded, letting the screen door slam as he joined them with the promised beers. He gave one to Adam and shoved a second at Frank before returning to lean against the house, his posture mimicking his brother's. "You have nothing to do with the decisions I made in the past or my lifestyle now, so get over yourself."

"Slow down there," Adam ordered, raising a hand for quiet. "Look, both of you need to take a deep breath and start again. Cam, you may think you're an adult and can make your own decisions, but trust me, having a family who cares about you trumps that independence, okay? So, get the stick out of your ass and talk to your big brother—he deserves your respect."

Frank coughed, then tipped his drink in a toast. "Much obliged." He turned toward the shadows where Cam scowled. "What my good friend said so eloquently is that I missed you, we all did. It's only natural to want to know where you went, how you ended up in the FBI, and most of all, why did you stay away?" He took a drink of his beer and set it on the railing. "You owe that to Momma, at the very least."

Cameron planted his considerable bulk in one of the wooden rocking chairs, which groaned under the weight. "I don't like talking about those days. You, Frank, more than anyone know how hard it was for me back then. I wasn't always this size," he said for Adam's benefit. "Being the skinny runt in a classroom filled with boys testing out their testosterone was hard—like real hard." He started rocking, the old chair creaking and grating with his movements, seeming to echo the anxiety of those days. He nodded at Frank. "I was labeled a fag—hell, even my own brother believed it—thrown in a locker, head stuffed down a toilet, you name it, they did it."

"I didn't care if you were gay," Frank growled. "Don't you get it? I was trying to protect you." He swore and straightened to pace the length of the porch. "You were coming home with black eyes and nosebleeds. What the hell did you think I should do?"

"Leave things alone?" Cam suggested sarcastically. "All you did was make things worse. I tried to explain that, but you were just like Pop—unyielding. It just fanned the flames. Those boys decided they were going to teach you a lesson—" He paused when Frank froze. "Ha, you thought I left because they were coming after me, didn't you? Well, brother-of-mine, I was nothing more than bait. Those Muldoon boys planned to tie you to the back of a horse and shoot it with an arrow. I overheard them bragging how that horse would run itself into the ground and you wouldn't have enough skin on your ass to cover your toe. They were sick and tired of taking a backseat to the great and wonderful Frank Stein. Can't say as I blamed them for that."

He sighed and leaned back in the chair. "I couldn't stand the thought of you being hurt because of me, so I left. And I stayed away 'cause I was too damn ashamed to come home. Does that answer your questions?"

Adam whistled through his teeth. "And I thought my family was messed up. You two need to rein in that superhero complex you've got going. It's time to kiss and make up, life's too short."

Frank ignored him—big surprise—and started down the steps. "The horses need to be checked on. Tell Maggie I'll be back in a bit." He strode away, spine straight, tan cowboy hat bobbing in the dark.

Cam sucked in a harsh breath and released it noisily. "Why do I bother?"

Adam rose and patted his shoulder as he walked by. "Because he's worth it." He stopped and looked over his shoulder at Cam's grim profile. "He never once stopped looking. Keep *that* in mind while you're judging him."

6

Dust swirled in mini tornedos across the barren field. Grit burned Cam's eyes and stung his skin, but he didn't stop to take cover—he couldn't. If he didn't make it across this old playground before the Muldoon brothers caught up to him, he'd die.

He glanced frantically around him, but the churning wind made it impossible to see. A brief flare of hope rose that it would do the same for his enemies, only to be squelched when first one, then the other two boys stepped out from behind the broken-down clubhouse on the edge of the clearing.

So close to freedom he could almost touch it; instead, he skidded to a stop and lifted his chin in a false show of bravado.

"What do you want?" he shouted, the wind carrying his words across the intervening distance and slapping his opponents in the face.

Stunned at his temerity, the brothers looked uncertain for a too-brief moment, before the oldest one, Joe, threw back his head and laughed.

"You're a brave one, I'll give you that," he chortled. "Ain't gonna save your scrawny ass none, though." He gave the other two a shove, urging them forward. "You're as dumb as your old man, wandering around when a storm is brewin'. No wonder he's dead."

Fury rose, blinding him to the danger. Cam put his head down and charged, hitting the youngest Muldoon in the gut and sending both of them to the ground. He raised his fists the way Frank had shown him and pounded on anything he could reach, arms, chest, face, and felt the thrill of victory when blood spurted from the kid's nose and mouth.

But then the two left standing joined the fray and the tables turned. Now it was Cam crying out in agony as sharp boots kicked at his legs and ribs while the boy he'd been hitting flipped him onto his back, sat on his thighs and pummelled his torso until there wasn't a single inch that went unscathed.

Drifting in and out of consciousness, Cam pictured his father as he'd seen him last, strong and proud on his horse, waving to his family before leaving for what would be his last day on earth. If only he'd warned him not to go. It was his fault his father had died, and now it was his turn...

"Leave him alone," a voice roared, hauling the Muldoon

kid off Cam's chest. Cam blinked, then closed his eyes, defeated. His brother had found him...

"Cam? Cameron, where'd you go?" Frank gave his chair a light shove, drawing Cam out of a past he'd tried to forget.

He shrugged the fog away and looked up at his brother. Even though there was only three years between them, Frank had always been decades older in capability. Experience and wisdom shone from his gray eyes now, making Cam uncomfortable in his skin.

"I was catching a nap, until you interrupted me. It's been a long couple of days." Years, really.

"Ma fixed your room when you first turned up, why don't you stay and get a good night's rest?" Frank took the twin of Cam's rocking chair, leaning back with a sigh.

"Sounds as though you could use the sleep. Running the ranch keeping you awake at night, brother, or is it the beautiful Maggie?" Cam refused to acknowledge the bitterness coating his words. Frank deserved to own the ranch, Lord knows he lived and breathed the place.

"I wouldn't turn down an extra set of hands, if that's what you're getting at." Frank turned his head to shoot him a look. "After all, you are a shareholder."

Stunned, Cam straightened. "What does that mean? I haven't even been here in years."

"I'm aware." Frank returned to his appraisal of the land. "Dad made the three of us equal owners with Ma having final say on crucial decisions."

Cam's throat tightened in response to the bombshell that had just landed on his chest. His father had included him in the most elemental way he could, ensuring the family remained connected through their roots.

"I... didn't know," he murmured, dazed.

"How could you? You forgot our phone number."

Frank's condemnation cut deep, intertwining with the guilt he already wore like a hairshirt. "It wasn't like that."

"Oh, really, Cam? How was it then?" Frank exploded out of his chair and stomped across the deck to the railing. He turned and glared, his eyes icy. "We were—are—your family, we deserved to know you were alive, man. Mom deserved to know."

Angered, Cam rose and faced his brother down. "See, this is why I stayed away. It was easier to let you think I was... rather than put all of us through this crap. You want answers I can't give. I'm not going there, Frank, even for you." His chin rose, eerily reminding him of another time he'd stood up to a perceived bully—and lost the battle.

Frank frowned and scrubbed at his nape. "Look, I don't want to fight with you. Hell, I'm still getting used to the fact you're here. Let's table this discussion for a later date, some-time when you do feel like unloading, okay?"

Nonplussed, Cam gave a short, sharp nod, surprised to feel his fingers digging into his palms. He was beginning to think what he needed was a flipping psychologist.

Frank gave an answering nod and pushed away from the

rail. "Well, morning comes early. I'm going to head in and get cleaned up. You coming?"

There it was again; the guilt trip couched in pleasantries. But, maybe, for this one time, he could go with the flow and see where it led.

"Right behind you, man."

7

Adam stirred in the cream and sugar he'd added to his coffee and surreptitiously kept an eye on the comings and goings of the tiny café. The entire town of Huntersville, Texas could fit into his Las Vegas neighborhood, although people here were much more friendly. And curious. He'd received his own share of furtive glances, the stranger in the crowd.

The décor was right out of the 50's with chrome dinette sets in baby blue with glossy white tabletops, cone-shaped light sconces, and a wall decorated with silver dollar coins beside an old-fashioned till. It reminded him of the restaurant in Tidal Falls that his buddy's family owned.

The street out front was also in a time warp, with hitching rails, angle parking—who did that anymore—and western-style storefronts done in rustic wood and brick. Three pickups rumbled by for every car, and most were filled with either feed or hay. Hard to imagine he was sitting in a hot bed for drug smuggling.

"There you are, I've been looking all over," Brianne plopped down across the table from him like a breath of fresh air. Her curly hair was held back with a cheerful yellow scarf that matched the sunflowers on her fitted dress, and big hoop earrings; yellow bangles completed her ensemble.

He looked at all the shopping bags she'd stacked on the empty chair and shook his head. "Did you have to buy the store out?"

She smiled good-naturedly and rested her chin on her cupped palm. "You want me to fit in with the locals, I need new clothes."

"As long as you didn't go overboard," he said sarcastically as their server appeared, coffee carafe in hand.

"Oh, yes, please," Brianne chirped, undaunted. "I'm famished, did you eat already?"

"Not yet." He waited until the middle-aged woman filled their cups, then asked about breakfast.

"All day, every day." She pointed toward the large chalk-board on the wall behind them. "Specials are there."

Adam exchanged an amused glance with Brianne and raised his brow. "Do you need a minute?"

"Can I just get a salad, please? Oil and vinegar on the side, if you have it." Brianne reached for the sugar and poured a third of the container into her coffee.

"I'll do bacon and eggs, poached, with multigrain toast,

thanks. And more sweetener," he added as the server started to move away.

"Ha, ha." Brianne smirked. "So, what's the plan, boss?"

He was her partner, not her boss, but Adam felt about a million years older than his peppy colleague. "At least now I know where you get all that energy from."

She pushed the container his way. "Everyone has a weakness. Come on, spill, what's yours, Agent O'Connor?"

What *was* his? The people he cared about. He'd do anything for his brothers-in-arms, Maggie—Amanda.

"I have a few," he said noncommittedly, then hurried to change the subject. "Are you prepared to go back to the bar tomorrow night?"

Excitement sparked in her pretty brown eyes. "I'm ready. I talked it over with Jenkins—Special Agent Stein. He's going to introduce me as his new buyer, an entrepreneur from Salt Lake City with ties to Canada—it's perfect."

Famous last words.

In his experience, if it seemed too good to be true, it probably was. "I don't like this, but we don't seem to have a choice. Clark hasn't found anything damning on the phone we confiscated, and Thomas has been on our case to come up with something we can use."

"SAC Thomas has something to prove, cut him some slack. His predecessor left big shoes to fill." She smiled as the server returned with their respective meals. "Mmm, this looks delicious."

Actually, her salad did look nice, plated in an artisan bowl and overflowing with spring greens, onion slices, mushrooms, cherry tomatoes, and peppers. His own plate was loaded with rashers of bacon, pan-fried hash browns, and perfectly poached eggs. There was that word again—perfect.

"How would you know anything about SAC Rhinehold?" Just saying her name sent his pulse skittering.

Brianne quit pouring oil over her greens to give him a contemplative look. "I may be a newbie but she's a legend among those on the training field. After that young boy was fatally wounded in his bedroom in Kansas City, Rhinehold was instrumental in the resulting sting that netted almost a hundred arrests across the country. Violent crimes are on the rise and much of it can be tied back to the influx of illicit drugs making their way into the hands of our vulnerable. Her efforts pulled more than twenty-five pounds of Fentanyl off the streets, enough to cause up to four million lethal doses. I want to be her when I grow up." She laughed.

She made it sound like a walk in the park, when in fact Adam knew the deep emotional toll the operation had taken on Amanda and her team. Things they saw could never be unseen. The dead and dying; someone's child, father, mother, sister or brother. All with promising futures until the bite of addiction swept away their will to care. The country's drug problems were reaching epidemic proportions. It felt as though they were fighting an insurmountable battle, but if not them, then who?

"Just focus on the here and now, you have a long way to go before you can fill Amanda's shoes." Brianne's eyes widened like those of a wounded fawn, making him regret his tone if not the unsolicited advice. "Look," he said, setting his fork aside. "I didn't mean to bite your head off, but Amanda would be the first to tell you, this job will eat you up and spit you out, if you let it. There are some damn good agents out there who suffer from PTSD. Trust me, you don't want to go through that." Maggie was still in recovery and would be for some time.

Brianne's gaze softened and she reached across the table to touch his hand, offering comfort. "I'm sorry, I wasn't thinking. Your partner is an amazing woman. After everything she went through, well... not many could have survived."

Adam turned his hand over and briefly clasped her fingers before letting go. He'd been defensive when she was only young and energetic. He hoped she was never placed in a position to lose that enthusiasm. Which is why he had to make sure she was prepared for any eventuality. It could mean her life.

He picked up his coffee cup and cleared his throat. "There are inherent dangers that come with being a woman agent, and in your case..."

"Black?" She said quietly, cupping her mug. "I realize the obstacles; I live them every single day. But—" she blinked long, dark eyelashes at him. "I'm trained to handle racial and equality barriers, Adam. Give me a chance."

It frustrated him that she should have to deal with the creeps that were part and parcel of their missions, but he had to trust she would know what to do—and this time, he would be there if his partner needed him.

"Umm, someone is staring this way," Brianne whispered, her gaze furtive.

Adam glanced around, expecting one of the men from Frank's ranch. There was a couple at the till paying their bill and chatting with the server, an older man waiting impatiently for a seat, and a dark-haired pregnant woman.

He shrugged and started to turn back when something stopped him. That hair, the stubborn chin... He rose, his heart thundering in his ears. "Amanda?"

8

Rivero shuffled down the narrow corridor behind the bulky prison guard, Wallace. The cuffs chaffed his wrists and ankles and the connecting chains jangled, announcing their presence to the other inmates in the ward. They lined both sides of the hall; arms peppered with gang tattoos wrapped around heavy cell bars and eyes dark with envy and malice.

"Playing favorites again, Wallace?"

"Rivero, man, you getting out?"

"Nah, he's a lifer. He ain't goin' nowhere." Peters scowled, fists clenching as he watched his approach.

Five years, seven months, nineteen days and eleven hours, every damn minute spent guarding his back. Not for much longer though. Soon this prison and all the scum within its gray walls would be a fast-disappearing smudge in Rivero's rear-view mirror. The Texas debacle had hit him hard. The bitch who'd orchestrated the whole thing was being taken care of, but it wasn't enough. He was sick and tired of counting on others to keep his business going.

Head down, determined to keep his cool while walking toward his freedom, Rivero smirked at the losers he was leaving behind.

"Whose dick did you suck, man?" Another inmate pulled a Gene Simmons and cupped his crotch.

Wallace shook his head and rattled the bars with his stick. "You don't have anything we want, Julio, give it a rest why don't ya?"

The fluorescents flickered and zapped with electricity, adding to the growing tension. "Just get me out of here," Rivero snarled, keeping his voice low.

But not low enough.

Suddenly, a canister rolled into the hall, smoke leaking from the seams.

"Smoke bomb, look out," Wallace shouted, covering his mouth and nose.

The guard following behind shoved Rivero's back, nearly bringing him to his knees. "Move it," he ordered, drawing his taser.

Heart pounding, Rivero leaned forward, protecting his vitals, and hobbled through the dense smog, trying to stay away from grasping hands. Alarms sounded, rebounding off the cement walls and reverberating in his ears. He gasped like a fish out of water, the smoky conditions making it challenging to breathe. Someone had to have put a price on his head, that was the only explanation. He'd spent years building up his creds within these prison walls; no one would try something like this without a worthwhile incentive. They knew he'd be merciless when he caught up to them. Their death would be used as an example; mess with Luis Rivero and pay with your life.

A grunt came from off to the left and he felt, more than saw, the guard go down. It was just him and Wallace now, against a group of rioting inmates with nothing left to lose—

"Argh," he cried, as something sharp sliced his skin. Pressing a hand over the injury, he swore and pushed on, determined to make it through the door at the end of the hall. Where the hell were the guards? The irony wasn't lost on him. A lifetime of avoiding the law and now they would be the answer to a prayer.

He could barely see Wallace. The smoke burned his eyes and nostrils, slowing his progress. Then they were there, only feet away from freedom.

He stumbled forward, desperate to escape, and realized too late there was more than one man in the hallway.

"I told you I'd handle it," Wallace rasped, turning his taser on Rivero.

"Change of plan, boss wants him dead," Peters said as though discussing the weather. He stepped around Wallace, who gasped and dropped the taser, a shiv sticking out of the side of his neck, and paced toward Rivero, a panther surrounded by steel and concrete.

Rivero broke out in a cold sweat, aware his time was over but not yet ready to meet his maker. "C'mon, man, don't do this. I have money, I can pay you." He lifted his cuffed hands and railed at fate. "At least tell me who's behind the hit. You owe me that much."

Peters' smile reminded him of a Henry Fuseli painting he'd seen in one of the Prison's library books.

"Think hard," he said. "You'll figure it out."

What kind of cryptic bull—

The electric shock came out of nowhere. One minute he was stalling for time, and the next he was doing the funky chicken on the stained cement floor. It seemed to last forever, but the chaos that greeted him when he came out of it told him it had only been a matter of seconds.

Working to unclench his jaw, Rivero angled his head sideways and took in the swarm of guards. Inmates were pressed against cells, cheeks kissing the bars, arms twisted backward, and legs spread wide as security patted them down and returned them to holding.

Two guards worked to staunch the blood flowing like a river from Wallace's neck, though it was obvious the bastard was gone. Rivero's own arm ached like hell, but he was basically ignored for the moment while some semblance of order was restored. He thought about getting up and creeping out while everyone was occupied, but his chances of making it weren't high. Better to wait for his lawyer to show up and move the process along.

Now that the excitement had died down, aches and pains were making themselves known. He shot Peters a dirty glare. Whatever shit was going on, he didn't want any part of it. Who was this boss guy? And why had a price been placed on his head? Rivero planned to find out, just as soon as he could vacate the premises.

"Get up," a guard growled, reefing him by the injured arm.

"Ow. What the fu—?" Rivero swung his gaze to the hulking brute standing next to him.

"Shut your trap, Rivero. This is your fault. Two good officers down because of you. Hope you didn't have a taxi on hold outside, it's going to be a long wait." The guard yanked him to a cage and practically threw him inside, slamming and locking the door behind him.

Rivero swore and turned as quick as the chains holding him would allow. "Hey, what the hell, man? You can't lock me up for this. I have release papers. Hey, are you listening to me?" He banged his cuffs against the rails to no avail. The guards had already left the cell block.

His forehead dropped to the cold steel bars holding him from the outside world and tears leaked from his eyes.

9

Tired after the flight and subsequent drive, Amanda pulled into the small town of Huntersville and searched for a restaurant where she could freshen up before continuing on to the Bella Vista ranch. She'd decided not to call ahead, preferring to make her explanations in person. It was going to be awkward enough, as it was.

The town seemed to have one Main Street and not much traffic, allowing her time to unwind and appreciate the brightly decorated storefronts. Springfield might have decked their shops for Christmas, but she'd been too focussed on fitting in to notice.

Here, it was quieter, more laid-back country than frenetic city—if not for the looming meeting, she would have found it peaceful. A place to raise children.

Angels trumpeted from the tops of power poles. Strings

of lights swayed over the street and blanketed the trees, just waiting for dusk to turn simple into enchanted. Stores beckoned early holiday shoppers with tempting window displays and piped Christmas music. And to top it off, a giant pine tree at the end of the street was covered in large multicolored balls and silver garlands.

A pickup backed onto the street, freeing up one of the angled parking spaces. Amanda tucked her subcompact rental into the spot before turning off the engine and taking a moment to unwind. Maybe it was a mistake not to have called Adam first. He was bound to be shocked. Angry even. Hopefully, not dismayed. She could take anything but that.

"Well, Little P, you're about to meet your daddy. What do you think he's going to say?" She rubbed the solid swell of her stomach and tried to quell the nervous butterflies telling her to run while she still could.

She took a deep, cleansing breath and opened the door, carefully easing herself from behind the wheel. Glancing up and down the block, she finally spotted what she'd been looking for; a café where she could get a cup of herbal tea and maybe a light lunch before driving out to see Adam and whoever else might be staying at the Stein ranch.

Even though sullen rain clouds churned on the horizon, it was a relief to walk on sidewalks not covered in slippery snow. A tall cowboy exited the coffee shop just as she reached for the door.

"Pardon me, Ma'am." He doffed his hat. "Here, let me

get that for you." He held the door open and stood aside so she could enter. "Have a nice day now," he murmured, giving her a friendly smile.

"Thank you," Amanda replied, clutching her purse. Between fighting her way up the ladder at the DEA and her own failed relationships with the opposite sex, she wasn't used to being treated with consideration.

The noise hit her first; the babble of patrons blending with the clatter of dishes and clang of an old-fashioned till. The décor was diner classique. A gold-veined mirror behind a long counter showed off delicious-looking tarts and cinnamon buns under glass domes. Customers lined the counter on swivel stools, reading newspapers and drinking coffee or tall glasses of soda with colored straws. Booths in robin's egg blue filled the outer wall, the table-to-ceiling windows letting light flow into the small area, with matching tables and chairs using up the rest of the space.

She felt like a bug on display, the pregnant stranger in town, though the stares were furtive. Tired, and not seeing any open seats, Amanda turned to leave, but was stopped by the server.

"Were you looking for someone?"

Amanda shook her head. "No, it's just me."

The middle-aged woman gave her a kind smile. "Well, it looks as though you could use a piece of Sally's peach cobbler. I have a table near the back, if you'd like?"

The simple compassion tightened Amanda's throat.

"Thank you, that would be lovely." She followed as the woman snaked around tables, her mouth watering at the delicious-looking plates of food.

Dodging a chair in the middle of the aisle, she looked up to catch a young woman with classically beautiful features gazing at her, but it wasn't the girl who stilled her steps—it was the man with her.

Adam.

Emotions hit her like punches in the training ring; joy, love, temptation—anger, regret, disappointment. Obviously, he'd managed to move on from their brief affair better than she had.

Spinning around, she bumped against a table, mumbled her apologies, and strode, head high, toward the front door. She was a stupid, stupid idiot. What did she expect? A joyous reunion with the man declaring his undying love and devotion for their new little family? This wasn't a romance movie; it was real life—and it sucked sometimes.

"Amanda, wait," he called, the chair scraping the floor with a nails-on-chalkboard noise that grated on her ears and had her picking up her lumbering pace. She'd never missed her pre-pregnant agility more than in this moment. He'd looked good—damn him—too good.

She shoved the door open and took two steps before he caught her, his hand firm on her shoulder.

"Amanda, dammit, stop for a minute. What are you doing here?" He tightened his grip, forcing her to face him.

His gaze took in every feature as though it had been years instead of months since he'd seen her last and her silly, foolish heart turned over and practically begged for his touch.

She could tell the exact moment he noticed her condition—and seriously, how did he miss it before? His eyes widened comically, and his hand dropped from her arm as if pregnancy was contagious or something. She would have laughed if it didn't hurt so much.

"Why aren't you at the ranch?" she asked foolishly, trying to get her swirling thoughts into some kind of order.

He shook his head and guided her out of the path of people walking past, arms laden with packages. "I can't believe you're here."

She frowned, her back to the wall, literally. Should she tell him the truth now that he was seeing another woman, or let him think she'd moved on, as well? Her pride answered for her. "I have business in town. I'm not here for long."

He scowled, his brown eyes inscrutable. "Is that a fact? So, if I *was* out at Frank's, you could have just avoided this awkward encounter completely, is that it?"

Why was he acting annoyed? She was the one who'd walked in on their little tête-à-tête. She was the one who'd been betrayed. He'd led her to believe... it didn't matter. She'd tell him what she'd come to say, and then go back to her new life with her challenging job, friends—and a baby.

"You better get back to your date. She might not appreciate you running out on her like that."

"My...?" He glanced over his shoulder, then raised a brow. "She's not my date, Amanda. Brianne is my partner. Maggie decided to take permanent leave and Brianne got the dubious promotion. We were just going over our notes and grabbing some lunch. You should join us."

No. Nope. Not going to happen. It was bad enough that she was carrying his baby and he didn't know anything about it; there was no way she was going to calmly sit over an uncomfortable lunch with him and his... *partner.*

"Maybe another time. It was good to see you, Adam." Just the thought of walking away from him for the second time sucked the air from her lungs, but he wasn't hers, and in the end, that's what it came down to.

"I wouldn't have taken you for a chicken," he said, blocking her escape by backing her against the brick wall of the neighboring business. "Who's the father, Amanda?"

She froze, hardly daring to breathe. This was it; she could either lie and walk away or tell the truth and change their lives forever.

"Maybe I could use some lunch after all."

ADAM GUIDED Amanda to the table where Brianne sat, curiosity lighting her doe-colored eyes. He had plenty of questions himself, but he knew his SAC—she'd talk when she was ready and there was no getting anything out of her before then. His gut screamed the baby was his, but until he heard the words there wasn't a damn thing he could do about it—except stew in silence.

Brianne rose as they approached, her gaze widening on Amanda's face. "SAC Rhinehold? It's an honor to meet you, ma'am. You're a legend at headquarters." She shook Amanda's hand effusively, then blushed and apologized. "I'm sorry. It's just that you're such an inspiration to women in this field. I can't believe I'm actually getting the chance to meet you in person."

Adam sighed and pulled out a chair for their guest. "Ease up before you scare her away, Morgan. She pulls her pants on same as you and me, one leg at a time." A visceral memory of him removing said pants while she was laid out like a buffet on Frank's dining room table had him taking his own seat rather abruptly. "Amanda is here on government business." Or so he'd assumed. Maybe, she'd actually come to see him. To tell him he was going to be a father.

Holy shit.

Amanda sank onto the chair and crossed her legs at the ankle in the lady-like pose he'd seen her do before. "Please, it's simply Agent Rhinehold now—Amanda. I transferred to a field office and took a demotion in order to prepare for Little P here." She absently caressed her swollen belly and Adam's heart squeezed.

"P?" he asked. Did that mean she'd chosen a name without his input? Disappointment and anger that she'd kept the child from him flattened his lips until a woman at the next table gave him a nervous look and he forced himself to calm the hell down. "Do you know the gender then?"

She laughed softly, the sound tickling up and down his spine. "P is for Peanut. When I had my first sonogram, the image reminded me of a peanut, so that became my name for the little gremlin."

"Is the child healthy?" he asked abruptly. He would support it either way, but for Amanda's sake, he hoped there were no underlying conditions.

"Adam, isn't that kind of personal?" Brianne cocked a brow and gave him a don't-you-scare-her-away glare.

Amanda's glance moved between them as though she doubted his explanation of their relationship. Fair enough; since it *was* kind of his M.O., what with his previous affair with Maggie and then Amanda, but he could have told her she'd ruined him for anyone else.

"It's okay," she said in response to his question. "My obstetrician warned me my age and hereditary factors increased the risk for the baby's genetics and giving birth, but so far everything is good."

Childish or not, he crossed his fingers under cover of the tabletop and vowed to look into getting her the best care available—just in case. He wanted to demand answers; why had she walked away from him? When was the baby due? Was she ever going to tell him he had a kid?

"How long are you in town for... Amanda?" Brianne smiled warmly, sipping her coffee.

The server arrived at their table and offered Amanda a menu. "You look as if you could use a nice cup of tea, love."

"Oh, yes. That would be wonderful, thank you." Amanda glanced at the menu and handed it back. "I'll have a salmon salad sandwich on whole wheat. Do you have herbal teas?"

The woman nodded, accepting the laminated sheet. "Camomile, peppermint, rooibos, ginger—"

"I'll take camomile," Amanda interrupted the spiel. "Have you eaten already?" she asked Brianne—ignoring Adam—as the server hurried away.

"Yes, Adam and I—"

"Can we cut the crap and get down to why you're here," Adam interrupted the women's social niceties. "I'm assuming it has something to do with the Renegade Resolvers?" It was obvious from her startled expression earlier that *he* wasn't the drawing card for her visit.

She glanced at the surrounding tables as though he'd just imparted a state secret before shooting daggers at him. "What is *wrong* with you," she hissed. "This isn't the time or place. The walls could have ears, you know that."

"You should have been in the CIA," he muttered, annoyed at being called to task.

"Yeah, well if I was, you and I wouldn't have..." She snapped her mouth closed on an audible hiss. Her gaze slid to a bemused Brianne. "I'm sorry. Your partner tends to bring out the worst in me."

Not always. He couldn't deny the volatile nature of their encounters. It lit him up from the inside out. He felt alive in Amanda's presence. His blood pumped faster, the air seemed crisper, his senses buzzed with life and vitality. She was the most exasperating, opinionated, irksome woman he'd ever met, but she mattered to him. And not just because of the baby.

"Our hotel is down the street. We can talk in private there." He threw some cash on the table to cover their bill.

"Can I get this to go, please?" Amanda asked as the server arrived with her sandwich. The woman shrugged and took the money to the cash register. The lunch rush was ending, creating an awkward lull.

Brianne chuckled and tapped the table with French manicured nails. "You two sure you aren't married? You sound like my parents. They butt heads all the time, even after thirty years of marriage."

"Trust me, she would sooner tie the knot with the devil than me." Adam pushed back his chair. "Shall we take this scintillating conversation elsewhere?" He was still reeling at Amanda's pregnancy, and Brianne's quips grated on already frayed nerves.

"If you don't need me, I have a few more things to pick

up." Brianne gave him a hurt glance before bending to gather her parcels, leaving him feeling like the ass he was.

"Give me those. How can you shop if your hands are full?" He took the bags and gave what he hoped was a conciliatory smile. "Try not to buy the stores out, will you?"

Amanda frowned. "Maybe we should wait until later? I'm rather tired after the flight and could use a rest."

She did look drawn. And anxious not to be alone with him. "Are you okay to be traveling... you know, like that?" He eyed her baby bump.

"It's a baby, Adam. Not the *Predator*." Just then the baby did a tuck and roll, belying her words. Immediately, her face softened and both hands cradled the infant. "He's active today."

She was so beautiful, she stole his breath. Then his mind caught up to what she'd said and he really was left gasping. "It's a... are you having a boy?" One with her chestnut hair and stubborn chin combined with his eyes and love of sports.

"Call me old-fashioned, but I asked my OB-GYN not to reveal the gender until the big day."

They'd made their way outside and Adam's time with her was drawing to a close. There was so much he wanted to know, but more than anything he didn't want to let her walk out of his life again.

"Let me help," he said abruptly, then hurried to add, "I can carry your bags to the hotel. You are staying overnight at least, aren't you?" Where earlier he'd relaxed under the normalcy of holiday shoppers and Christmas music piped into the streets, now he wished it all away. He wanted—needed—time to process what Amanda's pregnancy might mean to both of them. He didn't for one second consider the child as belonging to another man—she wasn't the type to fall in and out of relationships. She'd told him as much during their too-brief liaison.

She glanced between him and Brianne and he could guess what she was thinking. Brianne was a stunning-looking woman, but she wasn't for him and there was only one way to make that clear.

"Weren't you meeting up with Cameron for drinks later?" He didn't need to mention it was part of their under-cover op—at least not until Amanda explained the purpose of her visit.

Brianne's brow furrowed; understandably since he'd come down so hard on her after the bar fiasco, but then she caught on and nodded. "Drinks, right. Is it getting to be that time already?" She made a show of checking her watch. "I better hurry. Cam doesn't seem like the kind to appreciate tardiness." She smiled at Amanda. "It was nice meeting you. Hopefully we get a chance to chat before you leave."

With a last knowing look, she started off down the street, somehow managing to look like a model on a catwalk with an arm full of colorful packages.

Adam stared after her, wondering if he'd made a mistake.

She was too impulsive on her own. Maybe he should call Cam—

"You should go after her," Amanda said, interrupting his musing. He turned to see her backing away until there may as well have been a thousand miles between them.

"Amanda, stop. It's not like that…"

She shook her head, tears glistening on her cheeks. "I can't do this right now. I need some space. I'll call you tomorrow, okay?"

He frowned as she hurried away, leaving him alone with Elvis's *Blue Christmas* playing in the background.

10

Amanda woke from a restless sleep and blinked the strange room into focus. The quiet hum of an air conditioner under the window and faint murmur of voices in the hallway told her where she was before her brain came on board—a hotel room. In Texas. Near Adam.

She thought she'd been prepared but seeing him again had unleashed a tsunami of emotions she never expected. Leaving all those months ago had been the right decision though not easy. She'd broken regulations by having a relationship with someone under her command. And then, finding out she was pregnant... She admitted it was a mistake to keep her condition from him, but at the time, it seemed like the only thing she *could* do. Adam was a veteran of the DEA, with close to twenty years' service. It would have been wrong to jeopardize that because they'd made a mistake.

She rolled to her side and wrapped her arms around the

baby, the scar on her lip throbbing. "Don't worry, Baby P, Momma's got you."

The phone rang and her Judas heart fluttered. She sat up and made a grab for her cell on the bedside table with one hand while desperately trying to straighten her mussed hair with the other.

"Hello?" she said, despising the breathless quality of her voice.

"Agent Rhinehold, where's my sit-rep?" Director Kincade growled.

Amanda's stomach plunged. She clasped her robe closed over her chest and fought to clear her head of wishful thoughts.

"My plane was late arriving, sir. I've only been in town a couple of hours and... well, I needed time before approaching my old team members."

"Don't forget the reason you're there, Amanda. You have new priorities now." Kincade's voice was kind, if firm.

"Yes, sir. I'll arrange a meeting for tomorrow and be home the next day at the latest." After she spoke to Adam. "Have there been any developments from the break-in on my home?"

"We have a hit on a set of the prints found at the scene. Seems you've been annoying some powerful players, Agent."

Amanda rubbed her arm where a bullet had skimmed and left an ugly scar. She was well aware of the danger inherent in her line of work, but she'd always considered making the streets safer worth the risk. Mind you, she hadn't been pregnant then.

"—a mile long," the director was saying.

She frowned, realizing she'd missed important information. "Can you repeat that, sir?"

"I *said*, there were three separate sets of prints found and one belongs to a felon with a police record that's a mile long. He's wanted for armed robbery, resisting arrest, and this one's interesting, inciting a riot." Kincade cleared his throat. "It might be best if you stay where you are for the time being—"

"But what about the investigation I'm working on? I can't just roll over and play dead because someone wants me to stop digging into their affairs. Come on, sir, I can handle this."

He sighed. "Listen, I understand your determination, and even admire it, but with the rise in extremist activities I can't afford to have a mishap occur on my team that could have been prevented. You'll obey my orders until further notice—understood?"

Amanda glared at the serene print of a canoe out on a lake at dusk, loons floating past two fishermen without fear. She'd spent years facing her anxieties and now, because of the baby, she was being forced onto the sidelines.

"Can I at least work on my files from here?" She held her breath, hoping he wasn't going to place her on early maternity leave. She wanted—needed—to see this investigation through to its conclusion before then.

"Only if you keep me apprised of any, and I do mean *any*, new developments. I don't need a lone wolf under my authority. I like you, Rhinehold. You have potential as an Intelligence Research Specialist—as long as you allow the field agents to do their jobs. If you can't make that transition, I *will* cut you loose. There has to be substantiation of data or there's no chain of evidence. It's called working toward a common goal."

She winced, aware he was calling her out for jumping a plane to Texas. "Yes, sir. I promise to update you daily on my findings."

"And Amanda, take care of you and that child, as well."

Her throat tightened. "Thank you, Director Kincade."

"Oh, and before I go, a prisoner set to be released from Washington State Penn was knifed this morning."

"And?" Amanda asked, brow furrowing.

"Name's Rivero, Luis. Ring any bells?"

Luis Rivero, a drug supplier with ties to the Sinaloa Cartel, was the mastermind behind some of the shipments her DEA team tracked last spring. The threads were coming together, it was the big picture that was still blurry. But that's what she was there for; to figure it out.

"My team arrested two of his men in April, sir. They were attempting to ship cocaine and fentanyl via the stomachs of cattle coming through Mexico."

"I'm aware. We have people looking into a Teamsters Union now. I don't like coincidences. Keep your eyes open, Agent."

"Yes, sir, I will."

Setting the phone aside, she rose and strode into the spacious washroom. A spa-like bathtub with a sloped back and soft white porcelain finish was tempting, but instead she disrobed and stepped into the oversized shower, complete with marble tiles and a rainfall showerhead. Turning her face up to the spray, Amanda closed her eyes and allowed the water to calm her turbulent thoughts.

The stress of the last couple of years, beginning with Maggie Holt's captivity, growing tension and violence across the country, and her short-lived affair with a man she couldn't seem to forget, had her on tenterhooks. As a child, she'd worked hard to bring order to the turmoil of living with a drug addicted parent. She'd learned to sleep with a chair shoved under the doorknob in her room after one of her mother's friends tried to force himself on eight-year-old Amanda while her mother partied downstairs. It was then she became determined to stop the cycle. Take down the suppliers and the drugs would dry up. Even at that tender age, she'd instinctively understood the hierarchy of the drug trade.

A knock on the door interrupted her musings. She hurried to turn off the water and reached for a thick cotton bath towel. "Just a moment," she called, slipping into the hotel bathrobe. She'd asked for a wake-up call but hadn't expected door service.

Smiling, she tightened the belt on the robe and cracked open the door. "Thank you, I'm good ... Adam?" Her voice climbed an octave. "What are you doing here?"

He raised his eyebrows. "I'd think that would be obvious. We need to talk. Alone." His gaze did a slow glide from her face over what he could see of her robe and ended on her pink tipped toes. "Let me in, Amanda."

For one insane moment, she contemplated opening the door and throwing herself into his arms. It had been too long since she'd felt the comfort of a man—this man's—touch, but of course, she couldn't. Her natural reticence raised its ugly head and stopped her from making a fool of herself.

"I'm not dressed for guests." She raised the belt of her robe, hoping he would take the hint and go.

No such luck.

"I've seen you in less. Either let me in so we can have this out, or I'm going to serenade you in the hallway—your choice."

He wouldn't.

> *"Whenever I'm alone with you,*
> *"You make me feel like I'm home again."*

He would.

ADAM GRINNED as the door slammed closed and the locks disengaged. He figured singing The Cure's hit song would do the trick. What he hadn't expected was the punch to the gut when the door swung open.

Fresh from a shower, Amanda's skin was still damp—succulent came to mind. She'd wrapped her long tresses turban-style in a white towel, but a few rebellious strands had slipped free and curled lovingly along her neck. The robe, standard hotel attire, draped her figure highlighting luscious breasts, full hips, and a pronounced baby bump—Madonna come to life.

Her expression was anything but sweet and welcoming though.

"You never did listen very well," she said, moving aside to let him into the room.

He slid past before she changed her mind, breathing in the jasmine scent he always associated with her. His stomach clenched, memories of his face buried in her hair as she rode him to ecstasy tightening his core.

The room was humid, intimate, the bed unmade, messy, and still showed the imprint of her head on the pillow. He hadn't thought this out well enough. Meeting her in what was essentially a bedroom with his emotions running high wasn't wise. Angry as he was with her deception, he still ached to hold her in his arms.

Instead, he strode across to the window, threw back the drapes, ignoring a strangled cry from behind him, and cranked open the window with a view of the tired gray tarmac parking lot below.

"Do you mind much?" Amanda snapped, tightening the belt on her oversized robe.

She looked adorable with the material hanging almost to her ankles and a pout on those kissable lips.

"Not at all. You'll have to excuse me if I don't trust you not to skip town on me—again." He pretended nonchalance and perched on the edge of the sill. "I figure what we have to say to each other is best done in private." He shrugged and crossed his arms.

She lowered her gaze and made busywork straightening the covers before reaching for a bottle of pills on the nightstand.

Adam straightened. "Are you taking sleeping aids while pregnant?" He scowled.

"They're prenatal vitamins—recommended by my doctor." She shook one out and swallowed it down with the help of a glass of water, then collapsed on the side of the bed and stared at him. "Do you truly believe I would willfully harm this child?"

Did he?

No.

Even though Amanda placed her career above every-thing—even their relationship—his gut told him what his heart already knew—she was going to be an incredible mother.

"I'm sorry, I shouldn't have said that. Truth is, the baby is lucky to have such a competent parent. I bet you've read up on giving birth and child raising, haven't you?"

Her cheeks flushed but she held his gaze. "You know I like to be prepared."

And they had been, too. Obviously, his protection hadn't worked the way it was meant to. "I'm assuming you don't plan to give it up for adoption?"

Her eyes widened. "Of course not. I'm perfectly capable of caring for a baby on my own. Is that why you're here? To see if I've come asking for handouts?" She rose and pointed at the door. "I think you should leave."

He heaved out a relieved breath. Until this moment, he hadn't even been aware of how much he'd become invested in their relationship. If she was keeping the baby, he planned to be an active partner in the venture. He just had to convince one very stubborn woman he was right.

Closing the window so she didn't catch a chill, Adam sauntered across the room and stopped inches from those pink-tipped toes.

He lifted her chin and stared into hurt eyes. His tough, take-no-prisoners commander was showing her soft under-belly, and he liked it.

"I came here because I couldn't stay away," he

murmured, leaning to brush his lips next to the corner of her mouth though it killed him not to kiss her the way he craved.

She stiffened, then sighed, her warm breath a benediction on his face. "I'm glad you did," she admitted, swaying slightly.

He groaned, aware the admission hadn't come easy. "We're a pair, you and I."

Carefully, halfway afraid this was all a dream, he wrapped his arms around her back and pulled her as close as he could, reveling in the feel of the baby between them. "I never expected to become a father, but now that it's happening..."

"What?" she whispered, her gaze steady.

Suddenly uncomfortable with the depth of his emotions, he gave an awkward chuckle and took a step back, his arms dropping to his side. "It's kind of a big deal, that's what. We'll have to find a justice of the peace or at least a notary public—maybe the Chief can do it—and decide where we're going to live. You'll stay home with junior, of course, at least for the first while. I have money saved..." He petered out at the growing thunderclouds taking over her expression.

"Too much, too soon?" he asked like a big dummy.

She backed away until her knees hit the side of the bed, her eyes cold. "Too much ever, is more like it. This isn't the stone age, O'Connor," He winced. "If that was your lame attempt at a marriage proposal, it's no wonder you're single."

Placing a protective hand on junior, she sank onto the bed, her turban cockeyed. "Go away, Adam."

He stared down at her, tempted to force the issue, but she looked like a slight breeze would knock her over. Concern rose, though she wouldn't welcome that either.

"Okay, I'll go—for now. Get some rest and we'll talk about this later. I'm not giving up on us this time, Amanda, so you may as well get used to having me around."

Left with no choice, he kissed the top of her head and let himself out of the room, stopping long enough to take one last look at her dejected form.

Next time, he wouldn't accept no for an answer.

11

Amanda pulled into the Steins' ranch yard the next morning determined to do what she'd come to Texas to do, and then go back to the new life she'd made in Springfield.

End of story.

The classic farmhouse radiated charm with a wrap-around porch, dormer windows, sparkling white paint and black trim. She'd called ahead to let the family know she was coming and tooted her horn when they stepped onto the front porch to greet her. Magdalena Holt, Adam's former DEA partner, waved from under the beefy arm of her beau, Frank Stein. Beside them, Frank's diminutive mother smiled and said something to her son, who nodded and started down the steps.

He greeted her as she clambered out of the rental car. "Agent Rhinehold, good to see you again. Momma sent me to guide you up to the house. The ground can be uneven in places, we wouldn't want you to take a fall—"

"In my condition?" she prompted when he seemed to hesitate. "Thank you, Frank, that's kind of you. And it's Amanda, remember?"

"Of course," he said, bending a courteous arm. "Maggie is thrilled you're here."

"Really?" She hefted the shoulder bag over her arm and rested her hand on his muscular forearm. "I wasn't always her favorite person." It pained her to admit it, but she'd often used her rank to demand loyalty rather than earning her team's respect.

"Here, give me that." He grasped the strap of her bag and slung it over his shoulder as though it were a feather. "Adam called. He's running late but said to go ahead and start without him."

Amanda nodded and tried to quell the butterflies taking wing in her stomach. After their turbulent reunion at the hotel, she'd debated leaving him out of this meeting but what she had to say involved him, too, maybe even more than the others.

"How have you been, Frank?" She glanced sideways at the handsome SEAL Chief turned cowboy.

His lips quirked. "No lasting effects, if that's what you mean—and you?"

He was speaking of the concussion he'd received at the hands of cattle rustlers she'd been chasing for drug smuggling. Injuries he wouldn't have acquired if she'd been doing her job instead of falling into an emotional entanglement with Adam.

She stopped, her fingers tensing on his arm. "I should have come to the hospital to apologise, but I'm doing it now. You were kind enough to open your home to me and my team, and for that we endangered your family. I truly am sorry."

"Don't be," he said, patting her hand with his much larger one. "Thanks to your diligence, the poachers were caught, and I found my brother. I'd have to say I came out ahead of the bargain." He smiled. "Now, come up to the house before Mom and Maggie come down and tear a strip off my hide for keeping you to myself."

She chuckled, as she was meant to do, and continued up the hill, grateful for his assistance. They don't explain how unwieldy it is to carry a child in the baby books. Her body compensated for the weight, but it came at the price of a sore back and legs. The joy of childbearing. She grinned, absurdly grateful to be here, with people she'd grown to care about. It felt as though she'd come home.

"Watch those steps now," Emily—Frank's mother—called from the porch. "Frank, you keep a good grip on her. It's so good to see you, dear. Come, come, I've baked for the occasion. You're way too thin to be having a baby. Isn't she thin, Cameron?"

Amanda glanced up, surprised to hear the FBI agent's

name, and met his amused gaze. Frank's brother was a handsome man. Tall, with shaggy blond hair and piercing green eyes, he stood behind his mom, a hand on her shoulder.

"Ignore my mother, Ms. Rhinehold. She's a caregiver and tends to express her worry with food."

"And what's wrong with that?" Emily retorted, tapping his fingers. "I don't see you saying no to my pastries, young man."

"It's like he never left," Frank muttered, guiding her up the stairs.

There was an underlying bitterness in his words that troubled Amanda. She'd heard the story of Cameron's disappearance as a young fifteen-year-old boy and how it devastated their family. The not knowing for all those years would have been heartbreaking. She had a feeling Frank blamed himself. It would take time for him to come to terms with the fact that instead of being dead, his brother had become an undercover agent with the FBI and failed to inform his family he was alive. Whether he had a good reason or not, there was no excuse for putting them though that trauma, in her opinion. She hoped the Steins could work it out among themselves. One thing was for certain, she had enough problems of her own to deal with.

A car pulled into the yard just as they reached the top of the stairs and Amanda tensed. Apparently, Adam managed to tear himself away from the beautiful Agent Morgan after all. Then she castigated herself for the catty thoughts.

Maggie laughed. "If you could see your face right now."

Amanda forced herself to smile. "I have no idea what you mean." She hurried to change the subject. "It's nice to see ranch life is treating you so well, Agent Holt."

Maggie shared an intimate look with the man at Amanda's side. "It has its perks," she murmured before focusing on Amanda, her eyes widening a little at the closeup of her baby bump. "Are you planning on having that kid while you're here?"

A startled giggle erupted from Amanda's throat. "Scared to deliver a baby, Maggie?"

"You've got that right," she agreed, nodding. "I'd take on ten baddies before I became a midwife."

"It's not so bad," Emily inserted as Adam climbed the steps. "I helped bring plenty of young'uns into this world and it's a miraculous feeling." She smiled at Adam, who'd stopped way too close to Amanda for comfort. "Now that you're all here, let's go in so I can feed you and then let you talk about stuff I'm not supposed to know anything about. Makes an old gal feel unwanted, it does." She shook her head and started for the door, squealing when Cam wrapped his arms around her and lifted her feet off the ground.

"We'd be lost without you, Momma." He gave her a smacking kiss on the cheek, then set her down gently, his gaze going to Frank. "Isn't that right, big brother?"

A series of indefinable expressions passed over Frank's

face—love, brotherly pride, and... sorrow? Whatever they were, it made Amanda's chest ache.

Maggie must have noticed as well. She stepped between the Stein men and smiled winningly at Amanda. "I don't know about you, but I'm starved. I've been having the weirdest cravings lately. Must be all this fresh Texas air. How about we move this party indoors where Emily's delicious food is waiting?"

"Geez, Mags, when were you going to tell me you were pregnant?" Adam growled, looking fed up with women in general.

Frank froze, a granite statue.

Emily gasped, "*Madre de Dios!*"

Cameron clapped his brother's shoulder. "Congrats, man. You'll make a great dad, buddy. It's not like you didn't have enough practice with *moi*." He laughed.

For Maggie's part, she'd turned pasty. Concerned, Amanda reached out to grasp her hand in support just as Maggie's legs gave way and she crumpled to the floor.

12

A dam could have cut out his own tongue. What possessed him to say such a thing? If Mags had news to share, he was reasonably sure, as her ex-partner and best friend, she would have told him—whenever she was ready. Certainly not the way he'd blurted it out like a damn idiot.

He hovered behind Frank, who'd dropped to his knees and held a groggy Maggie in his arms, anxious to see if she was going to be all right. "I'm sorry, man. I didn't mean to freak anyone out. I assumed you knew, and, well..."

Frank shot him a lethal glance. "What? She's not yours anymore, O'Connor. Back off."

"I'm not a commodity, gentlemen. Now, let me up, please." Maggie squirmed to a sitting position, Frank's arm holding her steady. She gazed into his eyes, her expression tender but firm. "Don't blame Adam just because he's an idiot."

"Hey," Adam grunted, offended. "It's not my fault I'm perceptive."

"Is that what they call it?" Amanda murmured.

"Give the girl room to breathe." Emily clapped her hands and pointed at Cameron. "Run and grab her some water, will you, son?" Without waiting for an answer, she bustled forward and set the back of her hand against Maggie's forehead. Everyone waited until she smiled and gave the verdict, "No fever. Frank, help her off these cold planks and into the house. We need to get her warmed up."

"There's no need to fuss, really," Maggie insisted as Frank helped her to her feet. "It was just a dizzy spell. I'll be perfectly fine after a cup of tea."

Adam stood by helplessly while the Steins formed a protective circle around their newest member and hustled her into the house. Maybe he should leave. It wasn't as though anyone would miss...

"Are you just going to stand there wallowing in pity?" Amanda asked.

Startled, he turned to see her studying him, head tipped slightly, allowing thick chestnut waves to fall over her breast. He frowned. "I'm not *wallowing*, as you so kindly put it. I was simply thinking Mags looked tired. Maybe now isn't such a good time to talk business."

Amanda nodded, as though she completely agreed. "You

may be right, but the information I have can't wait. However, if you'd rather go, I can send you the bullet points later?"

Much as he wished to escape the awkward situation, it seemed he was doomed to ride it out. Releasing a pent-up breath, Adam shook his head. "Nah, if you think it's that important, I'd rather catch all the details now." He ushered her toward the open door. "Shall we?"

She smiled her approval, taking away the sting of Frank's dismissal. "Don't worry, Maggie's fine," she said, misinterpreting his reticence.

He realized in that instant it wasn't Mags he was worried about, so much as Amanda's opinion of him. Maggie was one of the strongest women he'd ever known. If she could survive the Mexican desert and months of torture at the hands of a madman, childbirth would be a walk in the park. Well, maybe not quite a walk, more like a long, painful marathon, but he had every confidence she'd come through fine.

No, the one he was truly concerned for was Amanda. The delicate blue veining fanning out from her eyes to her temples made her seem fragile. It angered him. He should have been there to make sure she ate right, got the rest she needed, driven her to doctor appointments—she'd taken that away from him.

He narrowed his eyes. "Are you seeing another man?"

If she'd gone from his arms to... Hell, he still didn't even know if he was the father. Adam's stomach plunged and he could feel the floor racing up to meet him.

"No," she snapped, cheeks flushing. "Not that it's any of your business."

"I'm making it my business." He grabbed her arm, stopping her in the entry. "Look, Amanda, I don't shirk my responsibilities. If that child is mine, I want to help."

Instead of the grateful look he expected, Amanda's expression darkened, and she jerked free of his hold.

"Your ego knows no bounds, O'Connor. I did just fine before you came along, and I'll be even better when you're in my past. Do you think we can get this meeting over with so that I can get the hell out of here?"

Adam stepped back a pace, disconcerted by her outburst. Where had his level-headed SAC disappeared to?

"Is there a problem?" Cam asked, poking his head out from the kitchen down the hall. His gaze landed on Amanda's defensive hands resting on her stomach and narrowed on Adam.

"Not anymore," Amanda replied, striding down the hall without a backward glance.

Adam raised his hands helplessly. "Women are impossible to understand."

Cam grinned. "You're just learning that now? I thought you were the womaniser in the Teams."

"Frank telling tales out of school, again?" He shook off his annoyance and headed toward the tantalizing aroma coming from the kitchen. "Something smells good."

Cam stood aside to let Adam pass, then placed a big

hand on his shoulder to hold him in place. "Momma made chili and cornbread," he said over-loud, before lowering his voice. "Have you spoken to Agent Morgan this morning?"

"Brianne? No, why?" Adam frowned, feeling as though he was wading through an emotional quagmire.

"She didn't show up at the bar. I sat there for close to two hours and nothing. I had to make excuses to my contacts. They expected to close the deal last night."

Adam pulled his cell from his pocket and tried her number. It went straight to voice mail. "It's me. Call when you get this." Maybe she'd fallen asleep after her big shopping trip and missed the appointment, but that didn't explain where she was today.

Amanda, Frank, Maggie and Emily stood at the kitchen island talking and laughing, a bittersweet reminder of what he was—the outsider.

"I'll check on her," he said abruptly. "Give my apologies, will you?"

"Let me go." Cam straightened. "I should have done it last night. Is she at the Green Tree?" he said, referring to one of the two hotels in town.

Adam nodded. "Room 208. Thanks, man. It's not like her to go off-grid." He hadn't worked with Brianne for long, but the DEA agent could normally be counted on to do her job. It should be him going, he was her partner after all, but Cam's concern changed his mind. The man wouldn't rest unless he did something proactive.

"I'll keep you in the loop," Cam promised, palming his keys. "Save me some chili," he called out to his mother before he strode for the door.

Everyone turned inquisitive eyes in their direction, and Adam was left to make excuses—lies really, because, of course, their mission was a secret. Sometimes, the deceptions were like an anvil on his chest.

13

A manda sipped her iced tea and finished off the last bite of key lime pie. "I'm so full, but I can't stop," she moaned. "Emily, your crust is sublime."

Emily smiled and set her own half-eaten slice aside. "Thank you, dear. We grow the limes ourselves. It's one of my favorites."

"Mine too, now." Amanda chuckled.

"You'll have to come back and try my pumpkin pie, maybe for Christmas?" Emily blinked innocently, her gaze going to Adam.

Amanda's neck flushed. Obviously, their secret affair wasn't so secret after all.

Adam eyed her warily over his own large slice of cream pie, as though expecting her to fly off the handle at any moment. To be fair, she deserved his censure; she wasn't acting like a sensible, level-headed agent, at all. Time to set her emotions aside and get on with the job.

"This was lovely, thank you," she said to Emily, reaching over to squeeze the woman's hand. "You've been both kind and generous to me and my team, even though we practically infiltrated your home. But, if I could just..."

"Borrow my house again?" Emily smiled. "Of course. How can I say no to my son's guests? You all stay, enjoy the pie, and I'll take Sugar for a walk."

The black lab at her feet thumped its tail on the floor and rose, tongue hanging from its mouth.

Frank shook his head. "That dog knows English, I'd swear it."

Sugar yelped her agreement—or maybe it was excitement when Emily pulled her pink leash off a hook by the back door.

"Labs are used in both the military and as police dogs. They're exceptionally good at sniffing out explosives, drugs, or weapons," Frank said, patting Sugar's shiny black head.

Emily's eyes widened. "Well, I would hope there's no need for her services here."

"Relax, Momma. Labs are also good companions, which is why Spencer got her for you. They're smart, that's all I was getting at."

"Well," she muttered, reaching for the doorknob, "you could have just said so. Come on, Sugar, let's leave these confusing people to their meeting."

Sugar eyed the countertop, her nose twitching for a wistful moment, then swung around and followed her mistress out the door.

Maggie chuckled. "You're in the doghouse now." She leaned over and stole a forkful of Frank's pie.

"Hey," he complained, then fed her another bite.

Amanda tamped down her envy and avoided Adam's gaze. She rose and took her plate to the sink, taking a moment to gather her thoughts. It was important she get her fears across to the people behind her.

Turning, she leaned against the sink, relishing the coolness on her aching back. "If you're ready, we'll get down to business." She waited for their corresponding nods, ignoring Adam's scowl. "I flew down because there have been some developments in the Rivero case."

"Rivero? I thought he was locked away?" Adam said.

She strode across to the table where Frank had set her bag. Flipping open the leather flap, she withdrew copies of the file she'd compiled. Keeping one for herself, she passed the rest to Maggie, who handed them out to the others. Amanda opened her folder and stared at Luis Rivero's mugshot. Forty-eight years of age, it was obvious from the grim, dark eyes and bold stance this wasn't a man to underestimate. A shaved head, tats down the right side of his neck—including a Roman cross under his eye—and tribal art covering both arms and pecs, he was an intimidating sight.

"Isn't this the guy the Finch kid tagged last spring for the drug smuggling ring we bagged?" Adam questioned, his brow furrowed.

"It is," Amanda agreed. "But it seems Rivero turned state's evidence on another federal crime and cut a deal with the prosecution. He was about to be released from prison three days ago when an altercation occurred, resulting in the stabbing death of a guard. Word has it, there's a price on Rivero's head. Our mission is to find out who is behind the hit, and stop them, before they finish the job. We need Rivero alive to testify."

"Why can't they keep him in solitary until the trial?" Maggie questioned, her gaze worried as it rested on Adam.

Amanda understood. She was concerned, as well. Especially with what she had left to share. "There's more, unfortunately." She stopped and took a fortifying drink of her iced tea, then turned to the next page in the folder, the one with a series of photos taken from her home after the invasion.

"What is this?" Frank asked, tapping the wanton destruction of everything she owned. Even now, a week later, it had the power to make her want to throw up. Not very professional, but then, she'd never been personally attacked before, either.

"Amanda?" Adam prodded, striding across the kitchen to take her arm. "You're shaking. Come sit down and tell us what's going on. Don't worry, we'll handle it together." The reassurance in his milk-chocolate eyes urged her to give in, turn into his arms and hide from the evils of the world. It wasn't like her to count on anyone for sanctuary, but with Adam she felt safe—cherished—and could feel herself blossoming under his attention.

Maybe it was the pregnancy, or maybe she was simply tired of being alone, but Amanda allowed him to guide her to a chair, conveniently next to his, and glanced up gratefully when he brought her a fresh glass of water. "Thank you," she murmured, before bracing herself for the barrage of questions soon to come.

"A couple of days before I flew here, to Texas, my house in Springfield was vandalized—in broad daylight." She waited a moment for the others to absorb the news, then carried on. "At first, I assumed it was a burglary, thieves looking for a quick haul." She leaned over Adam, her breast brushing against his forearm creating goosebumps down her spine, and pointed at the photo showing her overturned computer. "Until I found this."

"They left the computer?" Maggie asked, looking puzzled.

"It's gotta be worth a grand at least, right?" Adam didn't wait for Amanda's morose nod. He angled his chair toward her and took her hand in his. "What was on the computer, Amanda?"

Tears blinked into her eyes, blurring his handsome visage. "Names. My contact list, including agents I've known for years, some who are working undercover cases as we speak. All of you, as well. It's encrypted, of course, but any hacker worth his salt could figure it out with the right incentive." She brushed at the tears trickling down her cheeks. "My foolish mistake may have signed your death warrant."

Maggie gasped and turned to Frank. "This is all my fault. I never should have accepted your invitation to come here after my abduction."

Frank shook his head and bent to give her a lingering kiss. "And then I would have had to follow you wherever you went, because we are meant to be together. It's no use playing the blame game. We need to focus on dousing this fire before anyone gets burned."

"Frank, I appreciate your concern but you're a civilian now and therefore technically under my protection. I wanted you to hear this, because it may tie into an investigation I've been working on at the bureau that affected your SEAL Team a few years ago." Amanda lifted her gaze to Adam. "The Phoenix File."

Adam stared at her, perplexed. "Why are you examining something from a decade ago?"

"He's mobile again, isn't he?" Frank stared at her somberly.

"Who's... damn, it can't be." Adam rose and paced the kitchen, scrubbing his scalp in agitation. "How? I thought we'd destroyed his syndicate when I was in Iraq getting bombs thrown at me. This is ridiculous. The old bastard must be in his seventies by now and he's still a threat? Someone should have taken him out long ago."

Maggie's gaze ricocheted between Frank and Adam before turning to Amanda. "Who are they talking about?"

"Someone who thinks himself above the law—a four star general." Amanda kept her attention focused on Adam.

"Oh, my God. It's Baker, isn't it? Adam, he tried to have you killed." Maggie crushed the napkin in her hand.

Adam's mouth ticked up, though his eyes were steely. "I'm too miserable to die. It's Baker who should be worried."

"Where has he been hiding all these years?" Frank asked, rubbing Maggie's back.

"Would you believe right here in Texas?" Amanda flipped her file with a map of the state and an aerial view of the general's compound around so the others could see.

"Laredo?" Frank shook his head disbelievingly. "All this time and he was practically on my doorstep."

Adam swore and slapped his palm down on the table, causing the silverware to rattle. "Some ghosts just won't die."

Amanda empathized with him. She'd read the reports on the subterfuge he'd been forced to employ as a DEA undercover agent working to expose a multi-national crime ring within the military corps. Joining Frank's SEAL Team Five had been tough enough, but then, when he'd been discovered, and the team came under fire, he'd been coerced into faking his own death, leaving his teammates—brothers-in-arms—to pick up the pieces. It was then, after reading what Adam had gone through, that the Drug Enforcement Administration, the institution she'd always been proud to be associated with, fell off its pedestal.

"So, what do we do now?" Maggie murmured.

"We end this," Adam said, staring at the image of Baker's compound. "And this time, he goes down."

14

Winter wheatfields waved under a dying sun as Adam followed Amanda's taillights down the highway. They'd spent the afternoon going over the information she'd shared and were still no closer to a plan of action.

General Baker.

The first time he'd found out about the general's possible involvement in drug trafficking and sexual exploitation he'd been a newbie within the DEA. His previous SEAL training made him the perfect candidate for the overseas undercover work required. He'd been recruited to SEAL Team Five after rumors of a possible involvement with one or more of the members in the lucrative middle eastern drug trade. Instead, he'd found another transplant like himself, Tom Sheridan.

Sheridan—they didn't learn until much later—was

brought in by Baker to set up new connections between Iraqi smugglers and the Sinaloa Cartel in Mexico. A third-generation shipping magnate and powerful Massachusetts lawyer, Sheridan was the link between the cartel's drug cargoes and Iraq's gun running—and as a bonus, abducted young women were shipped from country to country as slaves or worse.

He rubbed his side where scars from the bomb that had gone off in an Iraqi village reminded him of the deadly stakes they were playing. They'd caught Sheridan in the end, though not without some hair-raising moments, but Baker and his syndicate had slipped away. The man had been a thorn in the Team's side for years.

And now, Amanda was involved.

It seemed far too big a coincidence that Baker happened to be in the same vicinity as the Renegade Revolvers, a quickly growing extremist group looking to overthrow the American government with criminal ties to Texas rebel rousers—and possibly Baker. He had to wonder now if that wasn't Baker's long-term goal from the outset—build on people's fears and civil unrest long enough and an uprising is bound to occur. Maybe the general fancied himself the new world leader. The real question was, did he plan to cause a civil war in order to accomplish his dream?

Amanda's blinker came on just as Adam's phone rang. He answered via Bluetooth and followed her into the grocery store parking lot on the edge of Huntersville.

"O'Connor." He pulled up next to her and motioned he

was on a call. She nodded and left him to stride into the supermarket, smiling as a cowboy doffed his hat and held the door for her. Adam scowled. What was it with these Texans and their chivalry anyway?

"Are you listening to me?" Brianne said impatiently.

"As soon as you start making sense, I will," Adam growled, out of sorts. He should have gone into the store with her. What if she needed help reaching something off the shelves? And she shouldn't carry her bags—how much was a pregnant woman supposed to do without it hurting the baby? He was sure he'd read something about...

"Agent O'Connor," blasted over the car's speaker system, jerking his attention back to the phone call.

"You don't have to yell." He disconnected from Bluetooth and put the phone to his ear. "What have you got for me?"

"Quite a lot, actually." Brianne's natural eagerness leapt through the airwaves. "After I left you and Agent Holt last night, I decided to return to the Pickled Pepper on the off-chance the men we had under surveillance returned, and one did—the guy I *borrowed* the phone from.

"This is where it gets interesting. He didn't see me. I was sitting in a dark corner near the exit, like you taught me. Anyway," she hurried on as though she could see his displeasure, "he met up with another guy, a stranger—I went back and questioned the bartender later on and he said he'd never seen him before. The conversation between them got pretty heated but I couldn't make out what they were saying. Then, they got up and left. I followed. I had to," she added, her tone defensive.

Adam shook his head before realizing she couldn't see him. "No, you didn't. As a matter of fact, you were under direct orders *not* to engage with the suspects." He rubbed the back of his neck in vexation. "You're lucky they didn't make you for an agent or you'd most likely be dead by now. Since you took it into your head to flirt with danger, where did they go?"

"That's the best part," she said, sounding subdued for the moment. He had no doubt it was temporary. "Did you know there's an old, abandoned airport east of town? They drove together and took off in a Cessna that was already there, waiting for their arrival."

Adam straightened. So, cellphone guy had some influential contacts. He'd have to press Clark into rushing the analysis on the phone Brianne had stolen. "Where are you now?"

"At the diner, why?"

"Because Cam couldn't get hold of you and came to town earlier to find you, that's why." Adam caught sight of Amanda's white blouse through the tinted store windows and opened his car door, preparing to help her with her groceries. "I've got to go. Call and let him know you're okay, then get a good night's rest. We're going on a road trip tomorrow."

"He's here, we're having dinner. Where are we going?"

"Laredo. I have an old acquaintance I want to see." Time to rattle some branches and see what fell out.

———

AMANDA GATHERED a few essentials from the grocery store shelves for her extended stay at the hotel. Her room had a small kitchenette and she planned on making use of the space rather than subsisting on a diet of restaurant and take-away meals. Little P had turned her into a fussy eater over the last few months, though at least she hadn't picked up on any of the bizarre cravings some pregnant women seemed to get.

"Finding everything you need?" A woman in the store's garden green uniform looked up from stocking a shelf full of assorted condoms, everything from the *Ultimate Pleasure Pack* to *All the Feels*.

"Umm, yes, thank you." Amanda stared at the multi-hued boxes and wondered if this was where Adam had gotten his supply before... Did they have an expiration date? They must, right? But if the stock wasn't rotated, it could explain what happened in their case. Should she ask? That would be silly, wouldn't it? Then again, if it saved another woman from an unfortunate—baby P gave her a warning kick, and Amanda smiled. "I have everything I need."

The woman nodded, her salt and pepper curls bouncing

with energy. "Children have a way of filling our lives with joy, don't they? Is this your first one?"

Amanda rubbed her belly. "Yes, seven months. I have a feeling this little one will be a handful."

"An active baby means an easy birth, or so my momma told me. Seemed to work that way for me, but then I come from good farm stock. From the look of you, I'd wager you're a city gal?"

Amanda looked down, trying to see herself through the other woman's eyes. Her clothes were good quality, but serviceable, she wouldn't exactly call them metropolitan. She did have a weakness for shoes though—she'd saved for three months to get the pair she wore now, even though they pinched with her newly swollen ankles.

"I am, yes, but I'm enjoying my time in your pretty little town. Everyone seems very friendly." She actually found it disconcerting. In the cities she'd learned to keep to herself, people were too busy rushing through life to chat with a stranger.

"Or nosey, depending on how you look at it." The woman chuckled. "Mary-Beth, nice to meet you, ..."

"Amanda," she supplied. "Have you lived here long, then?"

Mary-Beth checked the box she'd pulled from the shelf and threw it into the basket at her feet—mystery solved. "Goodness, yes. There are four generations of us in these parts. Can't imagine being anywhere else." She added a new box of X-Large to the others and raised a brow. "Makes a body curious, don't it?"

Amanda sputtered out a surprised snicker. "I guess it's not a case of one size fits all."

They shared a conspiratorial smile.

"Are you visiting someone in the area?" Mary-Beth asked, her gaze friendly.

"The Steins. Do you know them?" Amanda was grateful she didn't have to tell this nice woman the truth.

Her eyes lit up. "Salt of the earth, that family, every last one of them. Emily is one of my dearest friends. She was over the moon when her sons came home. You know, Cameron was missing for many years. He's a grown man, now. Such a blessing to have him back—and Frank, too, of course."

Amanda smiled and nodded, but took a step back, preparing to finish her shopping and leave before any awkward questions she couldn't answer came out. She should have realized the Stein family would be well-known in this area. Their roots ran deep.

"Yes, well, I better get going before my ice cream melts. It was nice to meet you, Mary-Beth. Maybe I'll see you again before I go home."

"That would be lovely, dear. I was going to say, that young man of yours looks a might impatient." She nodded toward the front of the store.

Amanda whirled around, surprised to see Adam waiting

near the tellers, arms folded, and head cocked in her direction. A warm thrill ran through her body, followed by a heated blush. Did he know she was standing in front of the condom display? He'd never believe she was making friends there. It wasn't like she was known for her casual conversations. Well, in for a penny, in for a pound.

She pointed to the box of X-Large Mary-Beth had just stocked the shelf with. "I'll take a box of those, please."

15

Rivero frowned at the two-sided mirror in the interrogation room at the prison. He was so done with this crap. He'd been promised a ticket out of the joint and it wasn't happening. Instead, he'd almost had a shiv stuck in his craw like that crooked guard, Wallace. Either things had to change, or he'd use one of his weekly phone calls to get hold of a news publication. They'd be more than happy to run with the story and make him famous along the way. A slow grin took over as he pictured his face plastered on every newspaper and broadcast company across the country. With what he knew...

"Wipe that smile off your kisser, this thing is a mess," his lawyer, Samuels, grumbled, striding into the room with a fancy leather briefcase in hand. He slapped the case onto the pitted steel table, popped the locks and pulled out a file folder before taking a seat with his back to the mirror.

"I don't have much time, so let's get straight to the point. The DA's office wants you to take the rap for last week's riot in which two guards were attacked and one died."

Rivero slammed his hands palm down on the table and got in his lawyer's slimy face. "Well, you better make sure that don't happen, or maybe that guard won't be the only one getting hurt, if you catch my drift."

"Are you threatening me, Mr. Rivero?" Samuels leaned back and worked to loosen his tie, his expression calm.

The composed look worried Rivero more than the man's words. They better not plan on setting him up for a fall—he wouldn't go quietly.

He glanced at the mirror and slouched in his seat. "Nah, just messing with you. It gets boring in here. You know how it is."

"Actually, I do not," Samuels retorted. He opened the folder and gave it a quick readthrough before giving Rivero his attention. "My client is a busy man, but he seems to feel you are an important asset to his cause, and therefore has provided me with the resources to make these charges disappear."

Rivero grinned, this was more like it. "So, what are you waiting for, an engraved invitation?"

Samuels's patrician nose rose an inch higher. "But, I must inform you, should you agree to this negotiation, there will be penalties set out at a later date. Are you agreeable to these terms?" He pulled a tablet out of the case and opened it to a contract with a bright red x where Rivero was supposed to sign.

Since he'd basically do anything to get out of this hell-hole, Rivero pulled the tablet over and etched out his name without bothering to read the fine print. It didn't matter anyway, short of killing his own mother, he'd already sold his soul to the devil long ago.

The lawyer took the tablet and the file folder, sealed them away in his lock-tight briefcase, and rose to knock on the door. "I'll be in touch." And just like that, he was gone.

"What, no hug?" Rivero called after him. He swallowed his ire and waited for the guard to unlock his feet from the table he'd been chained to like an animal. He had a good idea who was behind his release. There weren't that many men who could pull the necessary strings to get him out, but then there weren't many with his particular skillset, either.

"Whose palms did you grease to rate a legal beagle like that guy?" the guard asked, yanking him to his feet.

"Maybe I'm as rich as Elon Musk, you ever think of that? These chains hurt my ankles," Rivero griped as he was prodded down another lengthy hallway—at least this one wasn't lined with cells.

"Quit your complainin', as we hear it you won't be in them for much longer. And you thinking you're as good as the SpaceX guy is just plain hilarious."

The three guards at his back laughed uproariously, as though he'd told a joke worthy of SNL. Pricks. They didn't know nothing about Luis Rivero.

But one day soon, they would.

ADAM DROVE SLIGHTLY over the speed limit with classic rock playing on the radio. He'd been razzed by his companions but calmly informed them it was driver's choice and turned up the volume on the Eagles' classic "Hotel California". The four-hour trip to Laredo seemed to take forever, but then, he was anxious to see for himself if Baker was truly in the area. And if he was... well, it was long past time for a reckoning.

"Are we there yet?" Cameron grumbled from the rear of the subcompact car. "My legs are cramping."

"Does it look like we're there?" Brianne shot back. "Maybe if you hadn't gone all macho-man, you could have been sitting up front with plenty of legroom—see?" She stretched her legs out full length and lifted her arms above her head to make her point, releasing a contented sigh.

Adam glanced over at her and shook his head. "Do you have to poke the bear every chance you get?"

She tapped a finger against her mouth and pretended to ponder the matter, eyes bright with laughter. "He's so easy to bait."

Cam leaned forward. "So, what's the plan? Walk right up to the general's front door and inform him we know what he's up to and he'd better stop or else?"

Adam rolled his eyes. "Yeah, that'll work. No, I just want Baker to know we're onto him—if we can press him into doing something rash, we might get enough to take the bastard down. He thinks he's infallible. We're going to show him he's wrong."

"You're going to start a war, is what you're going to do." Brianne frowned at Cam's hand resting on the back of the seat near her shoulder. "Have you spoken to SAC Thomas about this?"

"About what?" Cam said. "We're taking a road trip to see an old friend, nothing more."

Brianne raised her brow. "And you really expect that to float after today?"

"After today it won't matter. We're going to be the incendiary spark that brings a criminal mastermind, who happens to be a four-star general, to his knees. The FBI and DEA will welcome any other alphabet organizations who want a piece of him, too. The goal is to rid our nation of these extremists before they can gather enough influence to destroy us all." Adam lowered the shade against the milky rays of the late morning sun and shot Brianne a glance. "If you're concerned with our visit, don't be. Thanks to Amanda's research we have enough cause to question General Baker, and

Cameron, here, is our FBI lead in the investigation, so we're legit."

"I sent in a request for a warrant to Judge McNeil yesterday. It took some persuasion, considering who our suspect is, but she finally agreed to a full search. My team should arrive shortly after we get there. I asked them to wait for my word before entering the property." Cam said, meeting Adam's gaze in the mirror. "Frank told me a bit about what you went through. I figured you needed a chance to face the man and maybe get some payback for what he did to you."

Adam gave a stiff nod. So many years of bitterness and anger were hard to swallow. For years he'd lived in the shadows, forced into a new identity thanks to the man who'd tried to ruin him. It would be fitting retribution if he could now return the favor.

"I'm not sure what all these undercurrents are," Brianne said, glancing between them, "but I do know we need to have all of our ducks in a row if we're going up against a four-star general. So, what's the plan, boss?"

She had a point. Adam had been running on adrenaline ever since learning Baker was within his vicinity. He'd had the vague idea of striding up to the man's front door and demanding an explanation before snapping on the cuffs. Obviously, that was unrealistic. A compound like the one they'd seen in the aerial photographs was bound to have a state-of-the-art security system, intercom operated gates, video surveillance, maybe even a cadre of guards on the premises. They weren't going to welcome a car full of strangers—especially government officers—up to the house for drinks.

They needed a way in.

16

Stewing, Amanda paced her claustrophobic hotel room. Adam had no right to leave her behind on what was essentially her investigation. He was taking the whole protective alpha man thing too far. She'd worked long and hard to build a case against General Baker, and now she was being left in the cold simply because she was pregnant.

Frustration ate at her. She felt like leaving this one-horse town and returning to Springfield where she was at least appreciated. Or had been—she'd missed her daily call-in to headquarters yesterday and could imagine Director Kincade's disapproval.

Stiffening her spine for the grilling ahead, she picked up her phone and put through the call.

"Director Kincade's office, how may I help you?" Mike, his assistant, said, sounding distracted.

"This is Agent Rhinehold. Is the director available to take my call?" Was it wrong to cross her fingers and hope he was busy?

"Hold, please. The director instructed me to put you right through."

Lovely.

"Let me guess, you lost your phone and couldn't get a new one until today," Kincade asked, his tone weary.

Amanda dropped her head and realized she couldn't see her toes—another milestone in her pregnancy journey. "Nothing as inventive as that, sir. Truthfully, I attended a meeting between an FBI agent and my DEA team—*old team* —out at the Stein ranch and it ran late. Again, I apologise. I'm normally much more organized than this. I believe my work history would testify to that, sir."

"I'll take your word for it, Agent Rhinehold. More importantly, how did the consultation go? Did you impress on your associates the steps we are taking to keep their safety our priority after the security breach?"

"I did, though they were more concerned with the investigation we've been running into the Phoenix File. Did you realize Adam O'Connor has a turbulent history with the general?"

Kincade let out a gusty sigh. "Yes, we knew, but it was confidential information. I couldn't release that piece of intelligence to you. And O'Connor shouldn't have either."

Amanda glared at her reflection in the mirror. "It wasn't

Adam. I found it during my research. He was under my command for three years and I didn't have the right to know his life was in danger?"

"Not in this case. O'Connor was part of a highly sensitive mission overseas several years ago with FAST. His assignment was to search out a suspected narcotics division acting within the military. We suspected a high-ranking soldier was behind the operation, but had no way to prove it. When Agent O'Connor got too close to the truth, a price was placed on his head. He barely escaped Iraq with his life and spent many months in recovery before taking on a pseudo identity—under your command."

At least now she had a thorough explanation as to why it always seemed as though Adam held a piece of himself back from their relationship. The closest she'd come to knowing the real man was in the final days of their affair when he'd opened up about his fear of failing. She'd taken it as a literal worry about the case they'd been working on at the time, but now realized it went much deeper into his psyche.

"Did he... did Agent O'Connor ever seek help? I mean, I know personal evaluations are done after every operation, but did he ever take it any further?" And why hadn't she delved further into her agents' backgrounds when they'd joined her team? She'd known Adam was a live wire right from the start, but had put it down to his can't-do-wrong attitude and absurd good looks—what kind of leader did that make her?

"Don't blame yourself for O'Connor's shortcomings, Amanda. He was trained to bury his issues and get on with the job as a Navy SEAL—it's who they are."

That didn't make it right. If anything, she might have associated his behavior with dangerous overseas missions, had she known he *was* a SEAL.

"Well, now that he knows Baker is in the vicinity, Adam came up with a plan to draw the general out. He's gone there now with his partner and the FBI agent leading the smuggling case that intersects with our investigation."

"Was that wise? If they tip their hand too soon the general will disappear again, possibly forever this time."

A fear she shared with Director Kincade.

"I believe they've covered their bases, sir. There's a warrant pending and an FBI unit on the way. I don't think he'll slip the noose this time." *I hope.*

"It's your career that will be on the line if they fail, Agent Rhinehold. Keep me posted." He clicked off and left her staring at her phone and praying she hadn't made the biggest mistake of her life.

A sudden knock at the hotel room door startled her.

She rose from the bed and hurried to the desk to draw her service weapon from her purse before edging up to the door. The spyhole showed an empty hall. Her pulse beat like a triphammer through her veins and her palms turned clammy.

"Who's there?" she yelled, hoping to scare a would-be assailant away.

"It's me, Maggie." Her face suddenly appeared in the viewfinder and Amanda sagged against the door for a moment in relief. This whole thing had her on edge.

She straightened and flicked the locks, allowing the other woman into the room.

Maggie took note of the gun and raised her brow. "Expecting company?"

Amanda reengaged the locks and followed her, carefully setting the 9mm on the desk. "Jumpy, I guess. What brings you to town?"

Maggie shrugged and glanced around the neat room. "Geez, do you ever let your hair down?"

Amanda stared at her, nonplussed. "What are you talking about?"

"Nothing, forget it." Maggie sank onto the edge of the bed, then just as quickly rose, and paced to the window to push aside the drab brown drapes and look outside.

"You're making me nervous." Amanda straightened the blankets and waited, uncomfortably aware of her apple shape compared to the other woman's svelte figure.

Maggie let the curtains swish closed and took a seat at the small dinette. "Why are you staying here instead of at the ranch? We have plenty of room."

Amanda joined her, sinking gratefully onto the second leatherette chair. "To be honest, I thought it would be too awkward considering your past relationship with Adam."

Maggie sighed. "It was a lifetime ago, get over it."

"Is he?" Amanda shot back, affronted.

"Is he what? My best friend. A great guy. A dumb ass. Yes, to all of those. He's also brave, kind, loyal... and sexy, but then you know that." She grinned.

Deflated, Amanda sank back in her chair and stared at the complex woman across the table from her. "Why are you being so nice? We don't like each other, remember?"

"That was then—"

"And this is now, I get it. You're much more gracious about *this* than I would be." She looked down at the basketball where her flat tummy used to be.

Maggie shook her head. "You didn't *do* anything wrong. Get that out of your head. Adam and I were over years ago. I've met the man of my dreams, and I think you have, too. The question is, are you going to let him get away?"

"I refuse to tie him to me because of Little P, if that's what you mean."

"Little P?" Maggie's brow furrowed.

"I call him/her Little Peanut until I know the gender, and I'm saving *that* for the delivery room."

"Mind if I ask why you're waiting, I mean wouldn't it be easier to know?"

Amanda couldn't believe she was talking babies with Adam's ex, but then again, maybe it was time to get over her petty jealousies before it ruined not only the tenuous friendship Maggie was offering, but possibly a chance to make her relationship with Adam work. Amanda's heart fluttered just thinking of the two of them as a couple.

"I guess I'm more superstitious than I thought. If I don't admit it's real, then maybe I'll be granted the gift of this child, even if I'm not worthy to be a mother, you know?"

Maggie's expression softened. She reached across the laminate table and took Amanda's hand. "Trust me, after taking care of our ragtag crew you are more than able to handle one teeny-tiny baby." She squeezed and let go, sinking back in her seat. "Besides, you won't be alone. I happen to know of a great guy who will make a wonderful dad, if you give him the chance."

"But what if that's all he wants?" Amanda blurted. "I mean, it's more than I expected, but I find I want the whole fairy-tale, the white knight, the castle, wedding bells, everything. Am I just dreaming it could be possible?"

"No," Maggie said, smiling. "I don't think you're dreaming at all."

More than anything, Amanda hoped she was right.

17

Adam crouched in the cramped quarters behind the driver's seat while Cameron, because of his extra height, was folded into the trunk. The only satisfaction Adam received from the arrangement was thanks to Brianne's ability to seemingly hit every pothole on the pitted driveway leading up to the main house. More than once, he caught a muffled thump and curse coming from behind the rear seats, and grinned.

It had been surprisingly easy to enter the compound. Brianne simply pulled up to the intercom, informed the distorted voice coming through the speakers that she was here to see General Baker on an important government matter, and voilà, they were on their way. Either the general thought himself invincible, or he knew they were coming, and the surprise was on the three agents. Adam hoped it was the first option.

The car slowed to a stop and Brianne whispered, "We're here," keeping her gaze focused straight ahead so as not to give them away too soon.

"Okay, get out, but leave the door open as though you aren't sure what to do. And don't forget to click the trunk latch so Cam can escape." Adam shifted, preparing to exit the moment Baker appeared.

"We went over it a hundred times. I don't see why Mr. Big and Tall can't get himself out. They come with release latches, you know." Brianne stepped out, away from the safety of the door and put a hand to her forehead to block the sun as she searched the yard. At the same time, she held the key fob behind her back and pressed the trunk button with exaggerated emphasis.

"It should have been a hundred and one," Adam growled and opened his door to join her. "What part of protect your core did you miss?"

"You're overreacting. He's not going to do anything that blatant. The general hasn't avoided prosecution this long by making foolish mistakes." Brianne lifted her chin and nodded toward the front door of the house. "Is that him?"

Was it? Adam hadn't seen the man in years, and even then from a distance. He'd shown up in San Diego during BUD/S training to give the teams a supposedly inspirational spiel on the satisfaction they would get from fighting the good fight, blah, blah, blah. Funny, considering the creep had been knee-deep in criminal activities even then. Rotund, with a jovial face and curly gray hair, he looked like everyone's favorite uncle—even with the MMA bodyguard by his side. That one could cause them some trouble.

"Did you bring the file?" the general called impatiently.

Brianne exchanged a confused look with Adam. "He must think we're someone else."

Satisfaction flowed through his veins like whiskey on a cold winter's night. "That's even better. If we can gain access to the house, short of brute force, he'll have to listen to what we have to say."

"And you thought I was foolhardy," she hissed. "Do you not see the bruiser on the stairs?"

"Well?" Baker growled. "I don't have all day. Get up here, then."

Adam grasped Brianne's elbow and pushed/guided her toward the walkway. "He hasn't recognized me yet. Let's go before he becomes suspicious." In a louder voice he called, "Sorry, sir, this one is awestruck. She didn't expect to meet a hero such as yourself." The words clogged his throat, but they had the desired effect. The general preened and smiled down at them benevolently as they climbed the steep steps to stop in front of his exalted presence.

"Hands out from your body," the behemoth ordered, eyes flat.

Brianne hesitated until Adam nudged her along. "Do what he says. We're not here to cause trouble."

"Mind explaining why you were hiding in the backseat,

then?" Baker asked pleasantly as his man impersonally patted first Adam, then Brianne down.

Adam froze, and not just because another man was cupping his balls, though that definitely played a role in his response. He narrowed his gaze on the general, fully expecting Baker to be staring at him with recognition shining from those pale blue eyes. There was suspicion, and a hint of humor at Adam's predicament, but little more than that, and he didn't know whether to laugh or curse. Obviously, he hadn't made much of an impression on the man all those years ago.

Ego deflated now that he'd been relegated to little more than a pesky mosquito, Adam opened his mouth to spout some sort of lame excuse when Brianne beat him to the punch.

Literally.

She turned and slammed her fist into his arm, the picture of wounded pride. "See? I told you it was a bad idea. I'm probably going to get fired for this, thank you very much."

Adam growled and rubbed at the bruise already forming. Did she have to hit so hard? "You're not going to get fired. It was a harmless prank. I'm sure the general has been in love before, right?"

Brianne's eyes widened comically, before she swallowed her protest and batted her lashes. "I'm sorry, sir. We're new recruits and just wanted the opportunity to meet you before... well, you know."

The guard dog had returned to his master's side and stared at them like they were lunch. Adam swallowed hard and turned his attention to the general.

"What she's trying to say, sir, is that there is a rumor going around that you may be retiring soon and when the opportunity arose to meet you in person, I persuaded," he winked at Brianne, "my partner to let me tag along."

"Well, now that you're here, you may as well come in for lunch. Escort my guests into the morning room, will you, Matheson?" Baker smiled, and Adam's blood ran cold. He knew. There was no way a man with that much power wouldn't have eyes on his enemies.

As Matheson prodded them into the house behind Baker, he wondered if he'd ever get the chance to meet his baby or tell Amanda how much he loved her. Cameron better not have dozed off in that trunk.

———

Amanda smiled as Maggie returned from the washroom for the third time since she'd arrived. "Get used to it, it'll only get worse."

Maggie groaned. "How can someone the size of a pea put so much pressure on my bladder?"

"Just wait until the pea grows into a watermelon." Amanda chuckled. "Dry toast and weak tea will help with the nausea, though I'm guessing you're almost passed that stage, are you?"

"I hope so, I just came from my first pre-natal visit, I'm twelve weeks along." Maggie walked over to the mirror, and, tightening the cotton T-shirt over her barely-there baby bump, swiveled this way and that, her gaze dreamy.

"I'm happy for you and Frank, you'll be wonderful parents." After the way she'd treated the other woman, Amanda couldn't believe they were sitting here like two old friends. It was... nice.

Maggie turned, her gaze sympathetic. "Have you and Adam had a chance to talk?"

Amanda shrugged. "He wants to help, but I expected that."

"Except you want more."

Amanda nodded, tired of denying her heart's deepest desire.

"Oh, honey." Maggie let go of her shirt and hurried over to wrap her arms around Amanda's neck. "You need to tell him how you feel."

Easier said than done. She could command a team and stand up for herself in the male-dominated DEA environment, but talking about her emotions was like scaling a ten-foot wall in heels blindfolded—impossible.

"I don't think I can," she whispered into Maggie's shoulder.

Mags grabbed her by the arms, forcing Amanda to meet her gaze. "Do you love him?"

Did she? He aggravated her to no end, rarely agreed with anything she said, was tender and caring when she least expected it, and the sex... ruined her for any other man. But it was more; something elemental between them that she'd never felt before and was afraid she'd never feel again. She was afraid Adam O'Connor was her Achille's heel.

"Yes," she said softly, then stronger, more determined, "I do. I think I always have."

"There, that wasn't so hard, was it?" Maggie grinned and flopped into the opposite chair. "When's the wedding?"

Amanda gasped and burst out laughing. "One declaration at a time, please."

"Trust me, once you two quit circling each other like dogs in heat—forgive the analogy—he's going to want to put a ring on your finger. Adam is a closet romantic, that picket fence is closer than you think."

Not so long ago, love and marriage would have been the furthest thing from her mind, but now, with the baby on the way and the possibility of having her feelings reciprocated, Amanda couldn't think of anything she wanted more. Well, world peace would be nice.

Her phone jangled out a text, the sound harsh in the pleasant aftermath of their chat. A foreboding chill slid down her back, and she knew before reading the message, it was going to be bad news.

Rivero is out

"Damn it," she swore, glaring at the screen.

"What?" Maggie sat up, her eyes going wide.

"Remember the drug bust last spring, the op we ran from the Stein ranch?" The mission that went sideways when she'd been shot, and Frank almost died—another life almost lost thanks to her bad decisions.

"Of course. We stopped a large shipment of drugs from heading to the streets and caught a couple of Renegade Resolvers at the same time." Maggie glanced at the phone Amanda was white knuckling. "What happened?"

"One of the key players, Luis Rivero, was released from prison. My contacts tell me he plans on making an example out of my team. He has to save face with his associates and decided our heads on a pike will suffice." Heartburn rose, cutting off her breath. How was she going to protect her baby from an unseen threat?

"Well, that's not good. What do we do now?"

Amanda stared at her, thrown by her casual attitude. "Oh, I don't know. Run for the hills, maybe? Why aren't you more upset?"

Maggie raised a brow. "Seriously? It's not as though this is the first time I've been stalked by crazed drug runners. It comes with the job description, remember?"

Only too well. "Maggie, look, about that—"

"Forget it, not your fault. If I'd followed orders instead of going rogue it wouldn't have happened—that's on me."

Maggie smiled, though her eyes were bleak. "Rivero has to find us first. Besides, he'll be too busy rebuilding his crumbling empire to worry about a couple of semi-retired DEA agents."

Amanda nodded, relieved to see the desolate expression leave Maggie's gaze. She wasn't about to remind her friend that someone broke into her Springfield home and had stolen the information they needed to track them down.

18

Adam was mystified by the General's morning room. He was surrounded by floral prints, delicate furniture, and potted plants of every description. How could a man who looked like a beloved grandparent and lived in a house out of *Better Homes and Gardens*, be a coldblooded killer? He'd grown rich on the backs of addicts. The drugs his organization shipped into the country created everything from homelessness to violence to death, and yet here it was all sunshine and roses.

"Have a seat and then we can get to the bottom of why you're really here—Agent O'Connor." Baker waved them to a chair at a table filled with plates of bright red strawberries, green grapes, assorted muffins, and cheese. Adam's stomach churned.

"So, you do remember." He nodded for Brianne to take a chair but remained standing himself—defiant.

Baker ignored him to sit at the head of the table—where else—and smiled at his young visitor. "Tea, my dear?"

Brianne slid Adam a nervous look before reaching for a blueberry muffin. "These look so good, do you mind? I missed breakfast this morning."

"Be my guest, that's what they're there for." Baker's smile grew, as though he truly enjoyed the company. It was ruined by the presence of an armed Matheson standing guard in front of the closed double glass doors. They were effectively trapped, mice caught in a monster's snare.

"How long have you been living here?" Adam demanded, fists clenched.

Baker waved a jam-tipped bread knife in his direction. "You're being rude—*sit* down."

So, the benevolent despot had cracks—good to know. He let the General have this win and took a chair next to Brianne, shooting her a *pay attention* glare. She took a big bite of a succulent strawberry in reply—annoying woman.

"I detest bad manners. Now you've decided to join me, we can have a conversation like adults. As to your question," Baker went back to spreading jam across his croissant, "I bought this piece of property some years ago from a young family who, unfortunately, had a bad turn of luck with the loss of their stock. But then, your Master Chief knows what that can be like, I understand." He sank blunt yellow teeth into the soft pastry and eyed Adam across the table.

Adam surged to his feet, incensed, and Matheson started

forward, hand on the firearm strapped to his chest. "You bastard. What did Frank do to you, huh? This vendetta you've been carrying out all these years, I don't get it. You're a fricking General. You took an oath, the same as we did, to uphold your honor and protect our country. What you're doing amounts to treason."

"Adam..." Brianne's gaze warned him to calm the hell down. How was he supposed to do that when the man practically admitted to betraying the flag?

"At ease, dear boy." Baker waved Matheson back to his post. "Our friend here has the unfortunate tendency to lead with his heart. It's the reason he never moved up from operations. To be an officer you need an analytical mind—rather like the young lady." He beamed at Brianne and Adam wanted to tell her to run.

"I may not have the experience my partner has, but I do know a creep when I see one," Brianne sweetly replied, and it took a moment for the general to realize she was talking about him. The altruistic expression morphed into one that looked more like he'd bitten into a rotten apple.

Adam chuckled. "Guess that logical brain of hers figured you out quick enough."

Baker threw the half-eaten croissant onto his plate and wiped his hands on a snowy white linen, staining the cloth red. "I find myself tiring of this conversation. Let's get down to business, shall we? What did you hope to accomplish from this visit to my private residence?"

"Your arrest, and the joy of watching you rot behind bars for the rest of your no-good life, comes to mind."

"Everyone should have a dream," the general replied. "I have done nothing and you have no evidence, Agent O'Connor. I suggest you take your fantasies and put them to better use."

Adam shook his head and helped himself to a slice of good old American cheese. "That's where you're wrong. You're not as invincible as you think. We've been compiling proof of your operation for a long time now. You've made mistakes and I plan to take you down."

"A plan is only as good as the paper it's written on. You should know that more than anyone. Files disappear all the time, as do the people we care about. Be careful, Agent, you're treading on dangerous ground. Defamation of character is libelous. I'd hate to tie you up in the courts for the next ten years, your pretty girlfriend might not wait that long."

"What girl...?" *Amanda*. He had to mean Amanda. Adam lunged across the table, crushing the food beneath his weight. It didn't matter, nothing did except getting his hands around the bastard's neck and choking him until his eyes bugged out of his ugly head.

Brianne screamed a warning just as Masterson grabbed his legs and pulled him off, his chin smacking the edge of the table and rattling his teeth as he hit the floor. The breath left his body in a rush. Before he could regain his senses, a heavy knee landed on the small of his back, and his arms and feet were hogtied behind him.

"You son of a—"

"Tut, tut, tut, there's a lady in the room. No wonder you have so much trouble hanging onto women," the general said, his penny loafers in Adam's line of sight where his cheek kissed the floor.

"Brianne, are you okay?" Adam couldn't see her from his position and sure as hell didn't trust the jackal and his accomplice to let her go.

"She's quite all right," Baker growled. "My man got a little rambunctious in his hurry to rescue me from your ill-advised attempt on my life—which is a capital crime, by the way. Your friend will wake up with a sore head and a black eye, along with a healthy respect for a man's fist, I dare say."

Adam cursed and tried to throw the heavy weight off his back, but only succeeded in tightening the zip tie chafing his wrists and ankles.

"Let him go, Matheson. I believe he's learned his lesson."

The shoes moved away, and the goon got up, leaving Adam to thrash around until he could roll onto his side. Brianne lay unconscious on the floor, her cheek scraped and swollen. Baker had resumed his chair as though the last few minutes never occurred, a dainty porcelain cup in his too-large hand.

"You're going to pay for this if it's the last thing I do," Adam swore.

"Hardly the first time I've heard those words. Those people failed, and so will you." Baker sipped his tea and eyed him broodingly. "You've been a thorn in my side for too long, O'Connor. I let you get away with it because I had bigger fish to fry, but lately, I find myself slowing down, thinking of retirement. Which leaves me with a problem."

The sound of a weapon clearing leather was the equivalent of a pin being removed from a live grenade. Adam's heart literally stopped before resuming sluggishly, as though it knew its time was almost at an end. Funny, he'd always expected to go out in a blaze of glory, not trussed up on the floor like a pig on a spit. His biggest regret was not having the chance to tell Amanda how beautiful, brave, and smart she was, and how lucky his son or daughter would be to have her guiding their way. How he wished his foolish pride hadn't gotten in the way and prevented him from following her to Springfield to declare his love and beg on bended knee that she give him a second chance.

Instead, he was reduced to a different type of pleading. "Look, you have me. Let Brianne go, she's nothing to you."

"You're wrong." The general glanced at the recumbent woman and his lips quirked. "I have… acquaintances who would be most interested in interrogating the young lady. And when they're through with her, well, let's just say the market is open and leave it at that, shall we?"

"I'll see you in hell," Adam spat.

Baker laughed, his stomach jiggling under the waistcoat

he wore as though he was a dignified gentleman. "But not today," he said, with a slight nod toward Matheson.

Adam closed his eyes, not to brace for his own imminent death, but because Brianne's loss was his fault, and he couldn't bring himself to watch her die.

Shattering glass and a loud crash made him flinch. For a moment, he thought Matheson's shot had gone wide, but then the shouts began to make sense and he opened his eyes in time to see Cameron storm the room in full tactical gear with what seemed like a battalion of federal agents on his flank.

"About time," Adam growled.

"Anyone have an apple," Cam replied with a grin before crouching to cut the ties on Adam's wrists as his men swarmed the room.

"Just get me out of this. Brianne needs a medic. Did you get it all?"

Cam nodded. "Crystal clear. Now hold still or you might be the one needing stitches. Smart move setting the mic in Agent Morgan's hairpiece. They didn't even look for it there."

"Wasn't me, that was Brianne's idea." Freed at last, Adam sat up and shook his arms out to restore circulation, his relieved gaze on his partner getting checked by a guy with FBI in bold yellow letters on the back of his jacket. Another two had Masterson on the ground, repeating what had been done to Adam short of the leg trusses—more's the pity.

Finally, his attention turned to General Baker. A flurry of feds surrounded the man as he was arrested and read his Miranda Rights.

"Make sure everything is done to the letter of the law. I don't want the old codger getting out on a technicality."

"He won't. We've got him this time," Cameron assured him.

Did they? Adam didn't like the complacent look on the general's face. Something was... *Amanda*.

How could he have forgotten?

"Quick, give me your phone," he demanded.

Cam took one look at the panic that must be radiating from his pores and hurried to draw the cell phone from his camopants. "What's wrong? You look like you've seen a ghost."

Or a nightmare from his past. If either Amanda or Maggie were injured, Baker wouldn't make it to prison.

Frantic, he tried to recall the number of the hotel and ended up calling information, cursing the fact his own phone was out in the car. By the time the registration desk patched him through to Amanda's room he was almost hyperventilating. It didn't help that the general watched from across the room with a smirk on his lips, either.

Ring.

Ring.

Ring.

No answer.

Jumping to his feet, Adam tossed Cam his phone. "Call Frank. Tell him to get to the hotel, quick. I think Amanda is in danger." He plowed through the agents, ignoring the grabbing hands and orders to stand down. Clasping the arms of Baker's chair, he leaned in close to his ear. "If you've done *anything* to hurt the women I care about, I'll come gunning for you, and no one is going to stop me."

Filled with helpless anger, he pushed away and hurried from the room.

manda perused the shelves at the Tiny Tots Baby Store. Maggie had convinced her they needed a shopping splurge to fortify themselves after the text about Rivero. She had to admit, it was working. Before now, she hadn't bought any outfits for the baby, preferring to wait until closer to her due date, but there were so many adorable choices her cart was quickly filling up. Who knew they made diapers that small? And the onesies; she was almost sure she'd grabbed every color they stocked and in a couple of sizes because they were simply too adorable to leave behind. She was going to pay a fortune to get these shipped to Springfield but didn't have the heart to return them to the shelves.

Maggie wasn't much better. She'd found the cutest stuffed bears and a gangly giraffe with a bow around its neck. And then there were the tiny cowboy boots, surely meant for a doll. If they kept going, they'd need a truck to haul it all out.

"We'd better quit. My credit card is going to revolt." Amanda chuckled.

"I need a drink. Want to stop at the café on the way back to the hotel?" Maggie wheeled her cart toward the cashier.

"Good idea. I can't believe I forgot my phone in the room. I wonder how Adam is doing at the general's house?"

"I don't think you need to worry. Adam can take care of himself, and if he runs into trouble, he has his new partner and Cam to back him up."

As they left the store with their packages and continued up the street to the little restaurant Amanda had visited the day she arrived, she sneaked a look at Maggie. "Are you okay with him having a new partner?"

She'd been jealous herself of the lovely Brianne, but Maggie had been Adam's partner for five years, they had a bond. One that was bound to be strained with the turn of events.

Maggie slid her a glance and shrugged, shifting the awkward giraffe under her arm. "I won't deny it stings a bit, but it was my decision. I'm not the same as before I went undercover. Sometimes, I still jump at my own shadow. And don't you dare tell Frank, he'd just worry. I'm getting better, but I know my time as an agent is done. Besides, I have new challenges to face, like how to change a diaper." She laughed and opened the door to the restaurant. "I'm famished, how about you?"

Amanda hadn't been hungry until she opened the door and the aroma of French onion soup wafted past her nose. "Starved."

They found a seat by the window and chatted until the server—a young teen this time—took their orders and brought tea for Maggie and a tall glass of lemonade for Amanda.

"Have you thought about what you're going to do after the baby is born?" Maggie asked, squeezing her teabag and setting it on the side of the little Brown Betty teapot.

"Not really. I mean, I assume I'll return to work after I find a reputable childcare, which could take some time." Amanda sipped her lemonade, savoring the pungent flavor. "I have a fair bit of savings set aside so I'm not in any hurry to go back. I'll make sure it's the right decision for me and baby P."

"And Adam," Maggie gently inserted.

"Of course," Amanda said too quickly, then sighed. "Truthfully, I don't really know what his part in all of this will be. I have to focus on us." She patted her belly. "We're a team."

"I get that, really I do. It's just that I know how much Adam wants a family. He won't let you down, trust me."

Amanda looked at her swollen tummy and refused to cry. It was too late. He'd already let her down by allowing her to walk away last spring. A baby wasn't going to change that. The only thing she could do was get on with her life and forget she'd ever been in love with an exasperating DEA agent.

Maggie's phone rang and they looked at each other for a moment, remembering the last call they'd received while together. She glanced at the caller ID and visibly relaxed, a warm smile stealing over her face. "It's Frank," she said, before answering in a low, throaty voice. "Hello, lover, did you miss me?"

The teasing smile died as she listened to what he had to say. "Okay, we'll head straight to the hotel. See you then. Love you, too."

She hung up and reached across to take Amanda's hand, causing a shiver to crawl up her spine as though the sun had disappeared behind an angry gray cloud. "Don't freak out, but there was an incident at the general's house. Adam is fine," she insisted when the blood leached from Amanda's face. "Brianne got banged up, but it's not serious. They're on the way to town now. Amanda, do you hear me?"

She heard, though the words seem to come through a tunnel. Adam could have been injured. The thought repeated itself on an endless loop until she wanted to scream for it to stop. The baby, sensing her agitation, rolled once, then lay still, waiting, waiting...

"I've got to go," she blurted, pushing to her feet.

"Yes, I told Frank we'd meet them at the hotel," Maggie reiterated, reaching down to pick up her bags.

"No, you don't understand. I need to get out of *here*, go home, back to Springfield. Now." The panic was rising fast. She couldn't see him again. It would be too hard. "Please, Maggie, help me to leave him."

Adam's best friend looked up at her, that stupid, beautiful giraffe hanging out of a bag, and slowly nodded. "Okay. If you're sure."

She wasn't sure of anything.

"I'm sure," she said, the lie burning through her heart.

20

The airport was bustling with tourists, some visiting Austin for the first time. And then there were the businesspeople, obvious by the starchy suits and briefcases as they hurried from point A to point B, tickets in hand. Adam ignored them, his attention on the stubborn woman arguing with a flight agent, a lineup of impatient people waiting behind her.

She looked tired, her normally coiffed hairdo sticking out at odd angles, a pile of bags at her feet. When Maggie had told him what Amanda was doing, he'd been hurt and angry. Until he realized she was running. And if she was running, there was a good chance she cared. Stubborn people like her wouldn't go down without a fight.

That's okay, he was strong enough for both of them.

"Amanda."

He knew the moment she heard his voice. She froze,

whatever she'd been saying to the frazzled attendant hanging in the air as she slowly turned, as though afraid of what she might find.

"Going somewhere, darlin'?"

She flushed, and he took that as a good sign.

"What are you doing here?"

The crowd's interested gazes ricocheted between them, but he didn't care. He was tired of hiding his feelings for this beautiful, complicated woman he happened to love with every fiber of his being.

"Well," he said, moving through the throng. "I figured if the mountain won't come to Mohammad…"

She put a hand on her curvy hip, a slow smile hovering on kissable lips. "Are you calling me a mountain, O'Connor?"

He was close enough to take her hand now, but he didn't. It was her turn to give up a piece of that tenacious independence and admit she needed him half as much as he yearned for her.

"I wouldn't dream of it," he murmured. "Were you really going to leave without saying goodbye?"

Her eyes filled with tears, and he almost gave in then, but this was too important. If she couldn't, or wouldn't, let him past her tough outer shell, they didn't stand a chance.

"I'm scared," she admitted.

"Of what?" Him? He wouldn't hurt a hair on her head, she had to know that, didn't she?

"Of this." She flapped her hands between them like a waddling duck about to take flight. "Us."

"At least you're admitting there is an us. That's a step in the right direction." He smiled, amused, and humbled at the same time.

"It's not funny, Adam. I don't know what to do with all these feelings bubbling inside of me." She stilled, her great green eyes burrowing straight into his soul. "What if you die?"

He gave in, he couldn't help it. Taking her into his arms, he held her and their baby and breathed in the sweet, clean fragrance he craved like air. "What if I promise to be around for a long time to come?" he whispered.

They both knew it was up to fate and she could be fickle, but it seemed to ease Amanda's mind. She leaned back and gave him a wobbly smile. "Are you going to kiss me, then?"

He wasn't a religious man, but Adam came close to falling to his knees and thanking the Lord for a second chance with this woman—his soul mate.

Instead, he tipped her over his arm in a grandiose gesture, careful not to hurt the baby, and planted his lips on hers amid a chorus of cheers from their audience.

"I thought you'd never ask."

EXCERPT FROM TIDAL FALLS- BOOK 1
WOUNDED HEARTS SERIES

Sara Sheridan tapped her toes with nervous anticipation, and when her husband turned away to network with the senator and his wife, she made her move. Excusing herself from her half-hearted discussion on the state of the economy with old Judge Perkins, she edged out of the dining room and hurried down the dimly lit hallway, ignoring the condescending stares from Tom's ancestors lining the walls in their expensive frames.

Knees quaking now she'd in fact committed to her plan, Sara slid the key *borrowed* from his nightstand into the lock, entered his office and pulled the heavy oak door closed. She Flipped on the lights and froze as his mahogany desk loomed out of the darkness. The pungent scent of his tobacco violated her nostrils, but she forced her stiff limbs to move across the room. She wanted nothing more than to run, fast and far. But couldn't, not yet. Rolling his heavy leather chair out of the way, she slid her fingers across the keypad to wake his computer. Password protected, she'd expected that. Pulling a list from her pocket, she started at the top, working her way down.

Nothing. Please, please, plea...

The screen changed, signaling success.

Yes.

Her eyes slid shut in a brief moment of gratitude. Then, knowing she had to hurry, Sara grasped the thumb drive Fiona had smuggled to her and plugged it in. A quick search brought no results.

Now what?

Frustrated, she entered random words from the password list.

Nothing. Nothing. Nothing.

Crap.

Covert stuff wasn't her forte. Her hand sweaty on the mouse, and her ragged breathing loud in the otherwise silent room, she keyed in one last word.

Phoenix.

The screen switched and a list of names, dates and times appeared. She'd done it. Excitement skittered up her spine. The download took the longest minute of her life. When it was done she shut everything down, replaced his chair and turned to leave.

A muffled thud out in the hall just about stopped her heart. She wasted precious seconds staring at the closed door wishing herself invisible, before frantically searching for a place to hide. There were heavy velvet drapes covering the windows, they'd have to do.

Praying her dust allergies wouldn't give her away, she hid between the folds, clenching the edges of the fabric in her hands and kicking herself seven ways to Sunday for leaving the key in the outer lock.

Sara held her breath when the door opened, praying it wasn't Tom.

It wasn't.

Belinda, Jessica's nanny, entered and sauntered across to the leather sofa along the opposite wall.

What was she doing?

After an extensive search among the pillows the nanny smiled in triumph, pulling a pink bit of nothing from between the plump cushions. She was just pushing the material into the cleavage of her skin-tight dress when Sara's worst nightmare came true.

Tom snarled from the open doorway. "What are you doing in here? I told you to go upstairs and find my wife. Our guests are preparing to leave."

He strode across the room and snatched Belinda up by the arm, jerking her against his chest. "What are you hiding?" Pushing her hand away he shoved his fingers down the front of her dress and withdrew the scrap of cloth still peeking from between her breasts.

"Tom, please. I only wanted to find those before the staff or your wife found them. Let me go. You need to get back to the party. Everyone will be looking for you." Though her voice betrayed her nervousness, she still flirted with him through her lashes.

He crushed the silk, giving a sneering laugh as he bunched his hand into her blonde hair. "Do you really think I give a shit if anyone finds some thong? I've told you before not to come in here without me. I won't tell you again." His voice was a dark omen in the twilit room.

He dropped his head to hers in a punishing kiss that swiftly changed to passion when Belinda's arms and legs wrapped around him as though she were riding a stripper pole.

After long minutes that seemed to last forever to Sara, she broke away with a sultry laugh and backed through the open door, her finger crooking a follow-me message.

Tom hesitated, his gaze scouring the room before he slowly followed, closing the door behind him.

Sara remained hidden; her heart pounding. Even though her husband's actions had long ago managed to erase any of the tender feelings they'd ever shared, it hadn't made this scene any less repugnant.

Finally deeming it safe she inched her way back to the door, pressing her ear against the smooth wood.

Silence.

She turned the brass knob, grateful it slid open and hurried to her room, her mind already filled with the next step of her crazy plan.

Escape.

Get your copy here

AFTERWORD

Reviews are the lifeblood of any successful author. Without you, we can't be heard. If you enjoy the story, please consider sharing on your favorite social media sites:

Please click here to post a review:

Amazon

BookBub

Goodreads

Thank you,

Jacquie Biggar

ALSO BY JACQUIE BIGGAR

Wounded Hearts Series

Tidal Falls

The Rebel's Redemption

Twilight's Encore

The Sheriff Meets His Match

Summer Lovin'

Wounded Hearts Box Set

Maggie's Revenge

With This Heart

The SEAL's Temptation

Secrets, Lies & Alibis

Mended Souls Series

The Guardian

The Beast Within

Virtually Gone

Gambling Hearts

Hold 'Em

Crazy Little Thing Called Love

My Girl

Married to The Texan- Box set

Blue Haven

Sweetheart Cove

Sunset Beach

Men of WarHawks

Skating on Thin Ice

The Player

Single Titles

Silver Bells

The Lady Said No

My Baby Wrote Me A Letter

Tempted by Mr. Wrong

Valentine: A Hearts and Kisses Romance

Mistletoe Inn

The Sister Pact

Perfectly Imperfect

ABOUT THE AUTHOR

Jacquie Biggar is a USA Today bestselling author of romance who loves to write about tough, alpha males and strong, contemporary women willing to show their men that true power comes from love. She lives on Vancouver Island with her husband and loves to hear from readers all over the world!

In her own words:

"My name is Jacquie Biggar. When I'm not acting like a total klutz I am a wife, mother of one, grandmother, and a butler to my calico cat.

My guilty pleasures are reality tv shows like Amazing Race and The Voice. I can be found every Monday night in my armchair plastered to the television laughing at Blake's shenanigans.

I love to hang at the beach with DH (darling hubby) taking pictures or reading romance novels (what else?).

I have a slight Tim Hortons obsession, enjoy gardening, everything pink and talking to my friends."

Subscribe to her Newsletter and follow her on these sites:

Amazon | Website | Facebook | Newsletter

Twitter | Pinterest | GoodReads | Bookbub